Winslow Hoffner's
INCREDIBLE
ENCOUNTERS

MICHAEL THOMPSON

THOMPSON ORIGINAL PRODUCTIONS LLC
BRISTOW, VA

Published by Thompson Original Productions LLC
Bristow, VA 20136

Library of Congress Control Number: 2018902682

ISBN 978-0-9799216-9-8

Written and Illustrated by Michael Thompson

Edited by William F. Kemp
Author Photo by Kara Thorpe
Beta Readers: Daniela Eidelman & Joseph Leo Hickey

Printing History

First Printing, March, 2018

Printed in the United States of America

For

Kathy Smaltz

*In whose classroom
these characters first came to life.*

And for

Laura Scott

*In whose classroom
they launched into new adventures.*

 ONTENTS

Gambo

ave ya ever stared straight inta the eyes o' death... and scoffed?" the old man asked. John Chaplain was so caught up in scribbling down the fisherman's words, he hadn't noticed the question. He was halfway into his interviewee's last sentence when he realized it was directed at him.

"Oh," he stopped himself. He looked up from his notepad and a bulging, ice-blue eye met him. He nearly jumped from his chair.

The fisherman's buggy, unblinking right eye quivered at him, awaiting reply. "Well?"

John froze for a moment in the old man's intense gaze. The walls of the living room warped and groaned, and the fisherman's dilapidated

3

houseboat rocked groggily in the stormy gusts. "I... I dunno," John finally answered.

The man huffed, then got up from his stool and hobbled into the kitchen. When he yanked at the small handle of his tiny fridge, the entire door detached. "*Dagnabbit*," he muttered.

The young journalist sighed and pressed the stop button on his recorder. *This guy's insane*, he decided. *And his claims are ridiculous. A monster fish? Please... News should be facts, not a crazy old fisherman's tall tales.*

John glanced outside. Rain slithered over the window, making the glass itself appear liquefied. He squinted past the distorted porthole and noticed just how extreme the storm had become. The rain fell so rapidly, it looked to be spitting up from the bay into the sky, where sudden flurries of wind carried the droplets in all directions. The fisherman's dwelling groaned as another powerful gust swept in and tipped it almost completely sideways. Knickknacks and furniture slid to the right along the inclining surfaces, including John's chair. Fretfully, he grabbed for the windowsill to steady himself. The old man didn't budge; he

4

simply shifted his weight accordingly until the structure swayed to become level again.

John had never been on a boat before, much less a *house*boat, and he didn't like it. He couldn't fathom how anyone could put up with the constant clamor — creaking and groaning — especially in this kind of weather. And of course, the endless rocking of the floor.

He glanced out the window again, this time at the shore. The sand was dark, sodden with rainwater. *That'll be fun to walk in...* John's gaze drifted to his newly-shined loafers.

After a long struggle with the refrigerator door, the old man finally gave up and propped it against its box. "Bah!" He tossed up his hand and returned with a soda in his fist. The beverage hissed as he pried up the tab. He licked the fizz that bubbled from the top, then took a seat on the stool in front of John. "Now, where was I?" As he talked, soda and spittle escaped the spaces in his mouth where teeth had fallen out. It landed on John's notes. The journalist cringed. He snatched a tissue from one pocket to wipe it away, then hand sanitizer from another.

The old man took another swig. "Let's see…" he thought aloud. More spittle. Aggravated, John repeated the process. Napkin, sanitizer. Then he shielded his notepad from the line of fire.

Why on Earth did they assign me to this story? John wondered. *Because I'm new, that's why. This is just a filler piece they dumped on the new guy.*

John turned his recorder back on, readied his pen to write, and waited for the fisherman to start speaking again. But instead, the old man just stared at him with his bulging right eye.

He finally spoke, "Chaplain, why're ya takin' notes when ya've got that recordin' doohickey wit'cha?"

John stared at him blankly for a moment, then answered simply, "I like to take notes."

"Well, don't. Ya've got yer whatchamagizmo recordin' me. So let it. And look me in the eye while I talks ta ya. Makes the story better." The bulbous eye quivered.

"Mr. Hoffner, I—"

"Didn't I tell ya ta call me Winslow?"

"No."

"Oh. Well, call me Winslow. 'Mr. Hoffner's' too formal. Got it, Chaplain?"

John opened his mouth to reply, but before he could answer, Winslow spoke again, "Alrighty then. See that storm out there? Imagine it ten times worse. That's what me n' Hank was sailin' in."

"Who's Hank?" John interposed.

"He's my first mate o' course!" Winslow yelled, as if it was common knowledge. "Chaplain, why're ya interruptin' me?"

"I wasn't trying to, I was just —"

"*Arg!* Now I've lost me train o' thought! Storytellin's a delicate artform, y'know!"

John pushed a shaky hand under his glasses and rubbed his eyes, waiting for the fisherman to refind his place. Winslow's eye quivered in recollection. "The waters were rough. It was like they was angry with us... attackin' the boat. Like big ol' fists tryin' ta knock us over. The skies was angry with us too, it seemed. Shootin' its lightning down at us, blowin' its wind at us. Then that full moon — she teamed up with the water and made these big ol' waves ta shove us back..."

7

John listened to the old man babble in his broken English, wondering if amid his ramblings a decent quote would emerge for him to use in his story.

Winslow went on, "Now that I think about it, I don't think the waves n' the wind n' the moon was angry at all. In fact... I think the elements were tryin' ta warn us about somethin'. Tryin' ta keep us away..."

John's eyes glinted at that last statement, and he snuck the line into his notepad. Winslow caught him.

"Chaplain! What're ya doin'?! Didn't I tell ya ta let the recorder do its job?!"

John wiped a few droplets of spit from his face. "Yes, but—"

"But nothin'! Recorders record. Listeners listen. Got it?"

"Yes, sir."

"Good."

"Can I ask a question though?"

" 'Course."

"What did the fish look like?"

"I'm gettin' ta that. Be patient."

8

Winslow cleared his throat, then opened his mouth to speak. He paused. "Blast it, where was I?"

"The elements were trying to warn you about something."

"Oh, right. They were, and we was ignorin' them. We pushed on through the swells. Don't really know why we decided ta take off that night; I could tell it was gonna rain. My knees told me so, n' my knees is never wrong. Maybe it was 'cause the fishin's been bad lately, I dunno. But fer whatever reason, we was there. Then, it hit us."

"What? An idea? A realization?"

"No, the monster. She ran right inta us, nearly capsized the boat!"

"Could you tell what it was at that point?"

"Naw. All I could tell was that it was a big one. And whatever it was, I wanted it on the line. So, I cast the biggest lure I had — me lucky silver one — n' sure 'nough she bit straight inta it."

John sat forward in his seat, awaiting the next part of the story, but without warning Winslow got up and walked away.

"Wait!" John called, louder than he anticipated. "What happened after that?"

"Hang on a sec, Chaplain, I'm outta root beer," the fisherman replied. He grabbed another can of soda from the broken fridge before sitting back down. John bounced his leg impatiently while the old man took a long intermission to gulp down his drink. He wiped some soda from his scraggly, gray beard and smacked his gums. "Dagnabbit, it's gone warm," he murmured.

"Please, Mr. Hoffner, continue the story," John pleaded.

The fisherman shot a studying glare at the journalist.

John remembered. "Please, *Winslow*."

"Alrighty," Winslow announced. "Here we go..." He held a pensive stare at the wall. "Blast it, where did I leave off?"

"The fish took the bait!"

"Oh, right. N' she took more than the bait, y'see. She pulled me right in too."

"Really?"

"Yeah. I didn't let go of the line neither. I could hear Hank yellin' somethin' at me like, 'Let go of the pole! Let go, ya bafoon!' But I just held on."

"Could you see it?"

"See what?"

"The monster."

"Oh, yeah," Winslow guffawed, but quickly became serious. "I saw her alright, and I ain't never seen nothin' like this afore. Her eyes were pitch-dark. No light shone in there—none even glinted off o' them. However, they seemed ta glow. I know that sounds strange, but they were... radiating their darkness outward. Black spheres with dark auras 'round 'em. Scariest peepers I ever saw."

"How large was it? Could you tell?"

" 'Course I could tell. She was 'bout the size of a Great White."

"Maybe it *was* a shark."

"Naw, this weren't no shark. She had a head like an alligator, body smooth n' streamline like a dolphin, a big ol' tail like a whale, n' four li'l webbed feet on her underbelly."

"What color was it?"

11

"Dark on top, light underneath."

That's a Great White's coloration, John thought. "Are you *positive* it wasn't a shark?"

"Yes, yes, I'm positive! I'm tellin' ya, I saw this thing with me own eyes! When her mouth opened up, I could see fire! Fire whirlin' 'round in her throat."

"A fire-breathing fish?"

"Aye, Chaplain. That gudgeon's breath burned so hot, the ocean couldn't douse it." Winslow realized he was standing just inches from the reporter. He cleared his throat and reeled back his intensity, then strolled, standing before a sliding door that led to a small balcony overlooking the waves. "It weren't no shark."

John was overwhelmed with amazement and skepticism. Nothing like what Winslow described existed. It was exciting and fanciful. The stuff of myth and legend. But it couldn't be real.

The certainty in the fisherman's words said otherwise. The journalist checked his recorder, making sure the light was still blinking. It was, thankfully, since his notepad sat beside it, untouched for some time now.

12

"What happened next?" John turned to Winslow for the conclusion of the story, but saw he had stepped out onto the balcony. John watched as the fisherman stared down the storm and dug into the shirt pocket of his dark flannel.

Smoke break, John assumed. He went to pause his recording, but stopped when, instead of cigarettes, Winslow took out a small, brass whistle on a chain. John tilted his head and squinted through the waterlogged window, as Winslow blew into the peculiar instrument a few times, finishing his tune with a bird-like trill. Thunder struck. Winslow surveyed the bay a while longer, nodded, then pocketed the odd whistle and came back inside.

The houseboat grumbled as Winslow sealed out the fussy howls of wind and caught the journalist's confused expression. Winslow pointed at him. "Care fer a warm root beer, Chaplain?"

John smiled. "No thank you, Winslow."

"Alright, then." He disappeared into his tiny, doorless fridge.

"I *would* like to hear the rest of your adventure though."

Winslow called back an affirmative noise from inside the fridge. He surfaced with a whole roasted chicken on a plate, which he set carefully on the counter, muttering, *"Almost dinnertime,"* before snatching the last root beer. He returned to his stool and took a seat before the eager journalist.

"Okay!" Winslow said. He paused, his expression turned pensive again.

"The monster pulled you underwater," John reminded him.

"Right! Anyways, the beast pulled me down. All the way down, toward the abyss—I reckon that's where she lives. It was dark n' shadowy all 'round, but I could still see in front of me on account o' her blazin' breath. She didn't have no gills, so I think her fire boils the water inta vapor, n' she gets by on the fumes."

John's face lit up with childlike wonderment.

Winslow continued, "I didn't have that luxury, y'see. I needed air, n' quick. Finally, I was able ta get on the beastie's back, n' I started pummelin' that thing best I could. She thrashed about, then let out this terrible roar that pulsed through the water n' hurt my ears..." Simulating the beast's maw with his arms and its teeth with his fingers, the old man threw open his hands and yelled, "*GRRAAAAAHH!!!*"

Thunder exploded outside and short-circuited the houseboat. John let out a half-gasp when the face of the monster took shape through the twisted illuminants of lightning and moonlight that cluttered the shady room. When he blinked, the frightening visage changed back into Winslow's hands. John released the startled breath he had sucked in. Eyes still focused on his listener, Winslow hammered his fists against the wall, and the lights buzzed back to life.

The fisherman coolly picked up where he left off: "I was punchin' her in the neck like ya'd punch a shark in the gills — but that didn't help, 'cause she had no gills ta punch."

John leaned forward, though he was already on the edge of his seat.

"So, I popped her one in the eye!" Winslow exclaimed, demonstrating his uppercut. "*That* did it! The monster thrashed again, then went swimmin' on upward. She soared outta the water, me on her back, and crashed onta the shore. Then,

15

I stood right up, unscathed. The monster had gone n' knocked herself out on impact."

"That's incredible!" John cheered.

The fisherman grinned at his enthusiasm.

"What happened to the fish?"

"Oh," Winslow laughed. "Well, we was evenly matched it seemed. Now that I was back on land it seemed only fair she went back ta the water. I gave 'er a push..." Winslow slurped some root beer. "Next I looked, she'd clawed back ta the waves and vanished. Hank docked the boat n' came runnin' soon after, askin' if I'd seen it." Winslow chuckled. "*O'course* I'd seen it! I rode the thing!" He finished his drink. "Me n' that fish had an understanding."

"Did you ever find out what this animal was?"

"Matter o' fact, I did research it... Hadn't been to a library in the longest time... I came 'cross only one other story of a beastie like the one I saw. One 'parently washed ashore some time in '83 in the Gambia. They called it Gambo."

"Fascinating," John said. A thousand more questions swilled in his mind, but before he could ask any, the recorder beeped, indicating the memory card was full. He picked up the tired

16

device, as Winslow chuckled, "Just in the nick of time, eh?"

"Looks like it. Thank you for sharing your story, Winslow."

"My pleasure."

John gathered his things and immediately started choosing the words he'd use in his headline: *Winslow Hoffner's Incredible Encounter with a Monster Fish!* Such an amazing tale. But was it only a tale? *News should be facts,* John remembered, and sank in his chair. This story was too amazing to overlook. People *had* to hear it. He shook his head, battling with his thoughts.

Winslow noticed John's frustration. "What's the matter, Chaplain?"

"Your story's incredible, but I don't know if anyone would believe it."

"Don't you?"

"I do, because I can hear it in your voice. The way you recount it, it's so *certain*. But, I don't know if I can tell this thrilling tale the way you can, with that *certainty*."

Winslow scratched at his knit cap, as thunder rattled the walls. After a moment, he said, "Why don'tcha follow me onta this here balcony?"

John looked confused.

Winslow picked up the roasted chicken from the counter. "Storm ain't slowin', might as well enjoy it."

The clouds were dyed deep indigo. John sat on a creaky, foldout chair on the balcony, while Winslow stood. A thin awning fluttering above barely protected them from the windswept rain. The roasted chicken sat untouched on its plate, save for a single wing John was allotted.

"All I can spare," Winslow said.

John glanced at the remainder of the meaty bird. He thanked him, shivered, and took a bite, tracing the fisherman's gaze across the dark, stroppy currents, before a familiar sound pierced the wind.

Winslow blew his strange instrument, whistling low, high, then low again. The clouds thundered in response.

"What is that?" John asked.

"Bosun pipe." Winslow whistled once more. Low, high, low, trill.

"But, what's it for —?"

A thunderous response, this time from below. The water's surface frothed. John's seat squeaked as he shot up, face ghostly. Winslow's massive right eye caught him. The icy blue iris gleamed like titanium through the shade. It blinked.

"Take a look at this," Winslow said.

Lightning arced. Water boiled. The fisherman heaved the leftover chicken over the railing as a great beast burst from the ring of foam, rising and roaring. Fire churned in her gullet, charring the meal as she snapped it up whole. John dropped his wing bone and gawped at himself in the monster's pitch-dark eyes, his likeness both swallowed and reflected, casted back at him from a deep and distant blackness like the soul of a wishing well. The image changed and rushed toward him as the eye seemed to flash, and steam hissed through the spaces in her gappy fangs.

"Told ya Gambo n' me had an understanding."

John couldn't find the words to respond. The beast went back under. A flicker of fiery light displaced the murk beneath the rippling surface, revealing a shadowed form unlike anything he'd ever seen: fifteen feet long, a head like an alligator, streamlined body like a dolphin, a tail like a whale, and four webbed feet.

Awestruck, John instinctively reached to take his camera from his pocket, but Winslow grabbed his wrist.

"The best stories are almost unbelievable," he said. "Now ya have yer certainty."

A massive tail tossed in the moonlit waves. The beast slipped back to the depths and into legend, as John beamed an excited smile.

"Go write up a thrilling tale."

The Trouble with Mermaids

n avalanche of scaled, silvery bodies tumbled into an icebox while one was flopped across a cutting board and promptly sectioned into thirds by Ken Keeley's flaying knife. His sharp blue eyes squinted and rubicund features tightened as he pried at a stubborn rib, which snapped in half and splattered the cook's arms with fishy juices. He uttered a low grumble and shook the glop away, then grabbed a rag and tended to the slime that coated his tattooed forearm carefully, as though polishing the dark, ink anchor and its encircled epigraph, *Tada gan iarracht.*

Ken chucked the rag aside and uncinched the apron from his round belly before taking a short trip from the kitchen to the main floor, popping a toothpick into his mouth and resting his arms on the bar counter, beyond which he spotted his fisherman milling around the restaurant.

Ken called, "Ye just *love* makin' me work with mackerel, don'tcha, Wins?"

Winslow Hoffner's gaze didn't stray from Keeley's wall of maritime portraits and curios. "Don't kill the messenger, Keel," he replied. "If ya got gripes, take it up with the bay." The old fisherman's right eye twitched as he surveyed the restaurant's beach-themed paintings, customer photos, and clamshell figurines with enormous googly eyes that framed a brand new centerpiece to the chaotic collage: a splitting wooden ship's helm knotted with rope that dangled shells and sea stars like a nautical dream catcher.

"Where in the world did ya dig up this'n?" Winslow asked.

"Bought it yesterday at an art fair. Thought I'd shake up the décor a tad. Y'like it?"

Winslow snorted. "It'd be easier ta put up a closed sign if ya don't want no one ta eat here, Keeley."

The cook's face flushed red. "Now listen here, you!"

Keeley's mother promptly cleared her throat to quiet her son as she swung around the counter with glasses of lemon water and orange juice in hand. She was small but speedy, with a bun of silver hair on her head and a gentle, thin smile on her face. She shuffled across the squeaky floorboards to the beachview booth to serve a lady and her young daughter, who was giggling and playing with a blue-haired mermaid doll. "Here y'are missies."

The little girl's golden curls bounced with delight as she accepted the orange juice.

"What do you say, Lily?" her mother whispered.

"Thank you, Ms. Muirin!" the girl beamed.

Muirin smiled. "O'course, m'dear. Yer fishsticks'll be out shortly." She patted Winslow's elbow as she him passed by, then gave her son a sharp poke in the arm, whispering, *Watch yer fookin' language lad, there's kiddies in 'ere!*"

Ken pinched the space between his eyes and sighed through his nose, as Winslow went on, "What happened ta the ol' seagull painting, eh?"

"Hm?"

"The gull, Keel, where'd ya put it?"

25

"That old disaster? It's in the trash, there's no room for it now."

Winslow scoffed. *"Dagnab..."* He swatted the shells that dangled beneath the faux dreamcatcher and took a seat at the bar.

Keeley stifled a bemused laugh. "I swear, Wins, ye've got the oddest sentimentality sometimes. Why, at the *slightest* sign of change ye—"

"How's about a drink, Keel?"

Ken eyed him a moment, then shook his head and sifted for a glass. Winslow sat back, jaw shifting as he traced the crisscrossed beams in the ceiling and took a deep breath of the thick, fishy atmosphere, impressed by how often Keeley's Bayside Eatery managed to smell more oceanic than the actual ocean. Ken plunked a heavy glass mug on the counter.

"No ice today. Gots sensitive teeth."

"What few ye got left." Keeley filled the mug with root beer and the fisherman chugged it. He set down his glass beside another tankard adhered to the bony hand of the only other patron at the restaurant, a snoring, scruffy-bearded man by the name of Sal Hurly, though most knew him simply by his nickname:

"How many did Sleepy have afore I got here?"

Ken shook his head. "He was out before I finished pourin' the first one."

Sleepy snorted and tossed, his free hand flopping onto a stack of papers from the Bayfield Messenger. *Winslow Hoffner's Incredible Encounter with a Monster Fish*, the headline read. The fisherman snagged a copy.

"Chaplain got on the front page...?"

"Musta been a slow week in Bayfield, eh?" Ken teased. "Wasn't enough torturin' *us* with yer stories, ye had to go and give the whole town an earful."

"Are you the man that saw the Gambo?" a small voice cheeped.

Winslow swiveled to see the little girl standing before him, blue eyes glittering with wonder. The mother, who introduced herself as Linda Cunningham, covered her daughter's shoulder and apologized, "I'm sorry about that, Mr. Hoffner. Her father just read her your story this morning."

"Did you really ride the fish? Was it scary? How deep could it swim?"

Winslow's throat bobbed at the barrage of questions.

"Lily, don't bother the poor man…"

"Naw, naw, it's alright," Winslow said.

"Well how's about that, Wins? Yer a local celebrity now!" Ken chuckled. He gripped his friend's shoulder. "That's what happens when y'go spinnin' those fairy tales to reporters."

Winslow's right eye bulged as his left one squinted. *"Fairy tales?"*

The phrase made Lily hop in place and lift her mermaid doll. "Have you ever seen a mermaid, Mr. Hoffner?"

"Mermaids, huh?" Winslow looked over his shoulder at Ken, then cracked a grin. "As a matter o' fact…"

John Chaplain balanced a tower of folders between his arms and chin, making an awkward trip down the hall to his boss' corner office, when a shoulder clipped him and sent the papers bursting from his arms like confetti.

"Sorry," John felt himself say automatically as he knelt to gather his things, then wondered why *he* was apologizing.

"Not to worry, mate," a slick voice returned in an Australian tongue. John took a quick glance at him, an editor he had yet to become officially acquainted with. Sunlight filtered through the murky window behind him and silhouetted his form, leaving only his faint outline highlighted with silver. "Nell Dunney," the shadow introduced himself.

John straightened up his messy pile. "John—"

"Chaplain! Right, right, I know you. You wrote that fish story everyone's going on about." Nell laughed, and for the first time since the collision, bent to join him on the floor. No longer backlit, John could see his face. His features were snow-colored: ashen complexion, slicked platinum hair, but his eyes were coaly-black. They skated over the flung papers, as he twisted a red lollipop between his teeth pensively. "More leads?"

"Uh, yes. Potentially, if Mr. Nguyen approves."

"Ah, cheery ol' Albert," he chuckled. "That's a good man, there. Always a softy for the newcomers."

John smiled. He continued arranging his papers back into their folders.

"Fire-breathing fish..." Nell murmured, lifting one of the documents that had fallen: an illustration of the monster John had photocopied from a library book. Nell rolled his lollipop over in his mouth as his smile widened. The edges of his teeth were dyed crimson. "That's a hard sell. Have to say you did an ace job writing it, though, Johnny."

"Thank you."

"Almost forgot it was a fluff piece." Nell stood, smiling, and patted the new journalist's shoulder. John realized he hadn't helped him with the pile at all. *Fluff piece?* Clearing his throat, he evened out his stack and went to his boss' door. A woman stopped him.

"Missed one."

John rested his folders on a table outside Mr. Nguyen's office to accept the misplaced paper. "Oh, thanks. I thought I got them all."

"Sure thing. It was wedged under the trashcan."

John frowned at the page. It was the illustration Nell had been looking at. John lowered the paper and set it on the topmost folder, catching glimpse of Nell in the distance, making small talk and laughing heartily, but soon refocused on the woman who had helped him.

She smiled, dimpling her lightly-freckled cheeks, then quickly became formal. "Becci Hamrin." She extended a hand. "I just started here too."

"John Chaplain." He returned a handshake. "Nice to meet you."

"I loved your story." Her strawberry hair swished as she looked over her shoulder, then leaned in close and whispered, "Fluff pieces don't make the front page, do they?"

John grinned.

"Yer mad, Winslow, mad!" Ken shouted.

Winslow folded his arms. "I assures ya, I'm saner than any."

"What, pray tell, *brought* ye to such a part of the world?" Ms. Muirin inquired.

Winslow shrugged. "Business matters. I was a young man then. Fishin' wasn't *always* me occupation, y'know."

Sleepy shot up from his nap, a line of drool waggling from his lips. "How much rum was the cap'n slingin'?"

Winslow raised an eyebrow. "Can't vouch fer the skipper, but I hadn't a nip."

Lily jumped in place a few times. "How'd she do it? Was it magic?"

Winslow grinned broadly. "Mighta been. The skipper thought it a coincidence or happenstance or what-have-ya. But then again, he mighta been a bit *beschwipst* as he'd call it. Too enchanted by his own special potions ta notice the *magic* happenin' in the waters below."

Lily's eyes lit up at the word.

"Aye," Winslow went on, "I'd say I was the most credible source aboard that day."

Keeley gestured to his friend with his thumb. "If there's *one* thing this bloke's famous fer, it's aggrandizement."

Winslow's buggy right eye flashed sideways. "Nice word o' the day, Keel! This moment was indeed a'grand! Fer as clearly as I'm lookin' at each o' ya now, did I see the set o' lady's fingertips part the water's surface. I was taken aback at first, o'course. Thought maybe someone had fallen overboard n' was reachin' fer help. But with the twirl o' her wrist, the clouds went dark on her command... and up opened the skies with a fierce peltin' o' rain that flung us forward n' back..."

Several other patrons had wandered into Keeley's Eatery. Before long, Winslow had amassed a small crowd whose *oohs, ahs,* and gasps were punctuating his every statement.

Mrs. Cunningham chimed in first, followed by several other eager pleads:

"What happened next, Mr. Hoffner?"

"How much did you see?"

"Did it have a tail?"

"Go on, tell us!"

"The next thing I saw was—" Winslow hacked. Graveled, he covered his neck and responded, "Sorry folks, me throat's a bit dry."

Sleepy hastily swatted Ken's arm. "Fer God's sakes, Ken! He's dry!"

Winslow's root beer was replenished. He took a massive swig, licked the foam from his scraggly beard, then continued, "Righto! Next thing I saw was the maiden's silver eyes flashin' at me like coins 'neath the currents. One o' the crewmen besides me started shoutin' somethin' like: *Meerfrau! Meerfrau!* then went sprintin' off down ta the lower deck.

"In hindsight I really shoulda followed the poor lush. Aye, thatta saved me some trouble. But I was too distracted by the fishgirl I'd just seen! Too distracted ta notice the masthead swingin' off balance in the wind, headin' right fer me..."

The crowd gasped as Winslow clapped his hands together. "*BOOM!* Off I went inta the drink!" He lifted his knit cap and parted his gray hair to show the audience a crescent-shaped scar on his crown. "Clipped me real good, see?"

Lily covered her mouth. "Did you make it out of the water?"

The room giggled.

Winslow scratched at his cap, "Hm, it's been a while, but if memory serves I made it out alright. Adrenaline kicked in—I had plenty o' that back

34

then—n' I clambered atop this big ol' log that happened t'be floatin' by."

"A log?" Ken interjected.

"Aye."

"What're the chances of that, friend? A bonnie branch just coastin' in outta nowhere?"

Winslow tilted his head at him. "I'd say a smidge better than seein' a mythical fishgirl, Keel."

The cook crossed his arms and chewed on his toothpick.

"So there I was!" Winslow proclaimed. "Adrift in a sea so far from home—the skipper hadn't noticed I'd fallen off the ship, y'see. I was all alone. Spent the next hour or so hollerin'... hopin' they'd come back..." Winslow's voice trailed. A fishstick crunched as Lily snacked, the only thing audible in the silent restaurant. Winslow stared off blankly, shaking his head at the memory. "The details are a bit foggy. So was the night. There's no way the crew coulda found me, if they wanted to..." He downed what remained of his root beer. "Anywho, I'd been through a lot that night, n' that log was seemin' real comf'rble ta me, so I curled up on the trunk and drifted off fer a spell."

Sleepy lifted his head and hoisted his tankard. *"Drifted!* Ha!"

Winslow smiled. "That's right. I awoke the next mornin' ta the squawks of a seagull. It looked a bit like—" Winslow raised his arm to Keeley's wall of paintings but froze midway. "Blast it, no visual aid."

Ken covered his head and groaned.

Winslow's face crinkled wryly. "Now, granted, the log wasn't ideal fer sleepin', but I awoke ta a particular ache. I was layin' on some rock now, smack in the middle o' the sea! No idea how I got there at first. Then, the oddest thing happened..." Winslow stood. His ice-blue eye swept over his still listeners, each face ghostly with anticipation.

Fully awake, Sleepy blathered, "Well? What happened?"

"Out with it, lad!" Muirin urged.

"How'd you get there?" Lily queried.

Keeley chewed on his toothpick and squinted at his friend, tapping his foot on the squeaking, knotted floor. "Surely, Winslow, there was a logical explanation..."

"Aye. It was the mermaid!" Winslow exclaimed. "When I saw her layin' on the rock beside me the memory came floodin' back!"

"*Floodin'!* Ha!"

"Aye, Sleepy. She was holdin' my head, n' combin' my hair with this odd little doodad that looked like a conch shell made of silver n' jewels."

Lily looked inspired. Ken looked incredulous.

"She saved me alright," Winslow nodded with certainty, then chuckled through his nose. "However, I thinks she'd started the storm in the first place ta try n' get me in the ocean with her."

Keeley frowned. "And why's that?"

Winslow flexed his arms. " 'Cause I was the strappingest young seafarer she ever laid eyes on!"

Keeley's face flushed red. He couldn't hold back his skepticism. "Oh-hoh, Wins. Now ye've really shown yer hand!"

"Whaddaya mean? It's the truth!"

"Come now, friend. Do ye honestly expect us to believe some pretty mermaid had the hots fer ye?"

Winslow snapped, "I never said she was pretty! We're talking about a flippin' fishgirl, Keel! She was scaly head to fin; her hair was like seaweed—!"

When Winslow noticed Lily holding her doll close, he retracted, "Erm, I mean, certainly she was breathtakin' fer what she was. We was jus' different species is all." He cleared his throat and adjusted his knit cap, lowering onto his barstool. " 'Sides, I only had eyes fer one miss, y'see. A girl by the name o' Anna Meria Lough. And I dare say, I've never crossed any creature as remarkable as she."

Muirin sighed. "Oh, Anna. So cutthroat n' kind, that gell." Her rosy cheeks buzzed in remembrance. "Just the sweetest pair, you two."

Winslow smiled. "Aye. So ya can all imagine how awkward this was, y'know, lettin' the fishgirl down easy. Lettin' her know I was already accounted fer. Not sure if she grasped what I was sayin' or not. Though I figured she might, since she up n' left me in the heat fer a while!" Winslow tapped his glass for a refill. "Ha! N' I thought landlasses had tempers!" The crowd chuckled as the fisherman moistened his throat. "So, I went n' dozed off a second time. N' when I came to, I was back aground somehow. Sky clear, wind cool. I found myself lyin' there in white sand, with nothin' but a couple fin n' handprints draggin' back inta the sea. The fishgirl had come through fer me after all."

The crowd was thrilled. Some of them clapped. Sleepy hurrahed before curling up on the counter. But Lily was the most ecstatic, hopping and cheering.

"Did you see the mermaid swim away? Did she change the weather again?"

Winslow thought hard. "Well, it was real early n' me head was swimmin'…"

Sleepy muffled a laugh between snores.

"But if I recall, there mighta been a hand twirlin' out o' the water in the distance, makin' the clouds part like curtains ta the most gorgeous, ruby sunrise I ever saw."

Lily beamed a huge smile as her mother thanked Winslow for the exciting tale. With the crowd dispersed, Keeley stepped around the counter to lean against the bar with his friend.

"Be honest, Wins," he whispered. "Do ye write these up beforehand or think of 'em on the spot?"

"I don't catch yer meaning."

"Come on," the cook nudged him. "At least admit ye were embellishin' fer the gell."

Winslow shrugged. "Alright, fine. Ya caught me. I added in the sunrise at the end."

Ken's eyes narrowed. "So yer tellin' me with *absolute certitude* that we may not be chattin' here t'day had that fishgell not taken pity on ye?"

"Oh, I thinks she always intended on rescuin' me. She was just havin' a bit o' fun is all. But, who knows. They's fickle creatures, y'know." Winslow winked as he removed his knit cap. "That's the trouble with mermaids, Keeley. Ya can never tell if they're pullin' yer leg."

The cook was about to make a comment, but paused when Winslow reached inside his jacket and retrieved a comb to style the wisps of gray atop his head. Keeley's toothpick fell from his mouth as the fisherman dragged the silvery, jewel-encrusted conch through his hair, then tucked away his peculiar tool, redonned his cap, and scurried out the door.

By the time Ken Keeley followed him out, the old man was rifling through the garbage and retrieving the seagull painting from the curb. Ken

40

shook his head. "Y'know what, Wins? You keep that."

The fisherman cracked a grin and nodded, "Thanks, pal." He tucked it under his arm. "But ya should know I was takin' it with or without yer permission."

"Aye, I figured."

Winslow ambled down the dock and loaded the painting onto his boat, then gathered the mooring line and waved to the cook from behind the guardrail. "Same time next week, eh!"

"O'course! Try and catch me somethin' other than mackerel!" Ken waved back. "And watch out fer mermaids!"

"In *these* waters?" Winslow chuckled. "Not a chance, Keel."

Charming Beasts

 piranha head with a mane made of tangled seaweed and antlers made of branch coral guarded the entranceway of the cramped shack from its lacquered, wooden plaque labeled, *Piranhalope.* In the frankenfish's sheened, amber eyes flashed the reflection of John Chaplain's inquisitive stare.

The journalist adjusted his glasses and jotted some thoughts in his notepad, then spun around at the sound of a door crashing open. Jumbled, wooden wind chimes strung with sand dollars clattered as the figure appeared:

"Greetings, mortal!" a stout, frizzy-haired woman strode in. Her arms fanned the sleeves of a purple shawl with fringes that resembled the flowing tendrils of a sea anemone. Her head was topped with a crown bedizened by periwinkle. "I am the Countess Milly Matterhorn! You have wandered into a plane of disillusionment and revelation! Be prepared landwalker, for what you see cannot be unseen!"

Milly stood inches from John's face. Her dark skin wrinkled around her moon-colored eyes, awaiting reaction. The journalist cleared his throat awkwardly.

"Um, nice to meet you, Ms. Matterhorn. I'm John Chaplain from the Messenger."

"Oh, John." Milly broke character and cocooned herself in her purple cloak. "Apologies for the showmanship, it's a part of the experience, you understand."

"Of course."

"Feel free to have a looksee."

John wandered. The floor and walls were decked with maritime artifacts: old compass gimbals, nautical knots, whistles. There was even an antiquated, patinaed anchor propped up in the far right corner of the shack.

But staggered between the intriguing historical displays were far less convincing taxidermies of supposed "monsters" like the Piranhalope. His stare rested on one of the beasts.

"Fancy the beasties, hm? Bayfield's home to some of nature's fiercest legends."

"So I've heard..." John shook himself free from his staring contest with a disturbing, cycloptic eel. "That's actually what I came to talk to you about." He turned to face Milly again but jumped when one of the mummified animals seemed to lunge at him.

"The Squid-Shark!" Milly declared, proudly hoisting a plaque that featured a dogfish body with tentacles in place of a tail. "A ghastly, elusive predator. My husband and I had to fight tooth n' nail to catch her!"

John squinted at it. "Looks ferocious."

Milly giggled. "I'm feistier, honey. Want a picture?" She posed with her trophy and beamed a grin, silver fillings flashing.

"That's alright."

"Well, feel free to wander. It's a big place."

John looked around the closet-sized shack. He sighed. *This is a dead end*, he thought, flashing back to his conversation with Nell. Embarrassed, he flipped his notepad shut and buttoned his coat. "Thank you for your time, Ms. Matterhorn."

"Going so soon?" The old woman's eyes twinkled in confusion.

"I'm afraid so. I need to find something substantial for my story." John tried to leave again, but Milly spread her arms, fanning her long sleeves to drape the exit.

"Don't go yet. There's a whole back room to see, dearie. Only for the bravest of souls, however..." She hid her mouth with her shawl, lifted the Squid-Shark, and made a snarling noise.

"Please don't take this the wrong way, Ms. Matterhorn, but I'm looking for something a little less... hot glued."

Milly lowered the trophy fish and raised her brow. "Are you calling me a fraud?"

"What? Oh no, ma'am, I'm just... in search of some *real* evidence. My editor wants me to — "

"Break an old lady's heart, apparently! Just 'cause you ain't got the capacity to open those pretty blue eyes of yours and *believe* for a change, you feel the need to shoot down *my* museum? *My* livelihood?"

John swallowed anxiously. "Not at all, Ms. Matterhorn. I wasn't trying to—"

"How could you say such a thing? Not real..." She hugged the Squid-Shark to her chest and sobbed. "This frightful creature ate my husband's leg!"

"I'm... wait, what?"

"Took hold o' him with her suckers and just gnawed away! It was his favorite leg, Mr. Chaplain."

"I'm... so sorry..."

She blew her nose into a handkerchief. "You think the Squid-Shark ain't real? Tell that to my poor, one-legged husband!"

An old man with a bristly, white beard stumbled into the museum from the back room. He hid his hand inside the sleeve of his black jacket and gripped his arm, falling to his knees and spouting curses at the ceiling. "Damn! Not a day goes by I don't relive the bloodbath! That godfersaken Squid-Shark stole my hand!"

"Dammit, Peter! I said *leg*, not *hand*!"

"We agreed on *hand* this time, woman! I'm sick of hoppin'!"

Peter pushed back his sleeve and rubbed his still-attached hand, then nabbed a captain's hat from a mannequin to cover his bald head and zipped his jacket.

"Lyin' to a reporter... Pretty sure that's illegal..." he muttered as he passed her by.

"We had him goin' for a second!"

Peter ignored her. "Lyin' to a friend of *Winslow's* no less!" A whistling breeze clipped the doorjamb as he headed outside.

Milly looked awestruck, wide eyes landing on John. "You know Winslow Hoffner?"

John opened his mouth to reply, but Peter spoke for him. "*Know* him? Why'd you think he came here?! The boy wrote a whole article on him. The old coot snagged some fire-breathing dolphin this time."

Peter took a moment to shake John's hand. "Enjoyed your story, son. Tell Wins I said hello."

John thanked Milly's husband awkwardly.

"I'll be at Keeley's," the man huffed, shuffling into the cold. He glanced back at John. "Pardon the misses; she was in the theater." The door thumped shut.

50

John turned to Milly, who stared ahead blankly, rubbing her purple shawl between her fingers. John chanced a moment to speak. He cleared his throat, and she blinked free from her trance and turned to him.

"I should be leaving now too," John told her.

Milly swallowed. She marched past him to the other side of the shack. "This way, Mr. Chaplain."

"But Ms. Matterhorn —"

"You want a *real* story don'tcha?"

John sighed. *I'm never getting out of this place,* he thought. He felt his feet step away from the exit and follow his guide. Milly flashed a silver grin and reeled open the black curtain that hid the back room. John stepped through, the small space was cloaked in darkness.

"Boo!" A finger prodded his back and he jumped, as the lights made a popping sound and snapped on. Milly giggled at the reporter's reaction and ambled around him, shaking her head in jest.

John blinked a few times and shielded his view from the buzzing fluorescents.

"Shoulda seen your face!" she squealed. "That's an old theater trick, dearie. Redirection."

When his eyes adjusted, John could finally observe his surroundings. Mounted on the walls and dangling from the ceiling, a collage of mangled, frankensteined nautical creatures stared back at him: a three-eyed barracuda, a puffer fish with a beard, a trout with fur.

More of the same, John realized. Suddenly the word *fluff piece* was echoing through his mind.

Over by a central desk, Milly was petting the head of one of her figures, a wide-mouthed bull frog with antlers and wings.

John was prepared to leave again. "This is the back room?" he said.

Milly glanced at him. "This?" she snorted. "This is where I do my taxes, dearie." She reached into the mouth of the taxidermied bull frog and retrieved a small key. Yet another black curtain was reeled aside to reveal another hidden door, this one flanked by the taxidermy of a top hat-wearing platypus that twirled a miniature cane and gestured grandly to the secret passageway. She unlocked the door to a second dark room. John cautiously treaded on, fighting the nagging memory of Nell.

"*Redirection*," Milly whispered to him excitedly as he passed her by, flowed through the creaky doorway, and stepped onto a groggy, wooden threshold. John coughed away a swirl of dust, and the final set of lights crackled on.

A far more organized, far less theatric set of authentic displays appeared. All were covered with glass boxes and labeled with cursive nametags.

John investigated. There were legitimate skeletons and artifacts he'd never imagined could be real.

"They're delicate, be careful," Milly said. Noticing his fascination with one, she grinned, adding, "I call that'n the *kitty-snake*. Can't rightly pronounce her full name."

To John, the skeleton resembled an oversized salamander, though its skull did bare some surprisingly feline characteristics. Its bones were articulated in a fearsome pose with cat-like canines and a pair of claws poised to strike. There were even flares of bone on either brow that mimicked sharp ears and accentuated the feline visage further. John's eyes traced its ribs until they transitioned into a long, serpentine tail that coiled beneath it, and landed on the specimen's nametag: *Tatzelwurm.* He jotted the name in his notes.

Incredible, he thought, finding the memory of his altercation with Nell had been drowned by wonder.

His skepticism crept back as he recalled the hoaxes of the main hall. But then, why wouldn't Milly showcase the more realistic collection first? John posed the question to her.

She shrugged. "Most folks, they weren't believin' me anyhow..." She rubbed her arm. "And one day all a sudden the papers started callin' me a hoaxer. Killed my business. Then, when I decided to give 'em what they accused me of, they called the place *'charming.'* A roadside must-see for Bayfielders and tourists alike." She strolled ahead by a set of filing cabinets. "Bayfield forgot its history, but those Piranhalope T-shirts kept the lights on."

John's eyes flashed. "You have material on Bayfield's monsters?"

Milly smiled. "Courtesy of your pal Winslow I do." One of the filing cabinet's heavy drawers rolled open, filled to the brim with monstrous teeth, scales, treasures, and artifacts, all carefully labeled in plastic bags.

"These were all donated by Winslow?"

Milly giggled. "Half the museum was donated by Winslow."

John looked to her, astounded.

"The half that's real, that is."

"I can't believe Winslow found all this."

"Oh, he *lived* it, dearie."

"I thought Gambo was the only one he'd seen…"

"Oh goodness no," Milly laughed.

John's mind swirled with questions as he examined the drawer. He came up with an old, compass-looking instrument. "What's this?"

Milly giggled. "You managed to pick out the *one* trinket I know the least about. It belonged to Winslow at one point. Gave it to me when he said it 'wasn't no use to him no more.' Thought I'd like it. It's for navigation, I guess; that's all I know.

'Course I can't even figure out how to open the darned thing."

John rotated the sealed bag containing the brassy, octagonal casing. Its rounded top was imprinted with a raised emblem resembling the planet Saturn. On the underside was a piece of tape with the word, *Cryptolabe* scribed on it. He returned it to the drawer.

Next, Milly treated the journalist to a stack of newspapers from another cabinet, dating back to the mid-seventies. "You'll prolly find these interesting." John knelt to the floor and scoured through them, flipping to highlighted pages. Blurry images of serpentine monsters, massive tentacles, and trident-shaped tails decorated every issue. Milly leaned back in delight as she watched the headlines scroll over the reflection of John's glasses:

Creature Sightings Spark Intrigue, Historic Hoax or Pre-Historic Relic?, Unknown Animal Spotted Again Offshore, Do Monsters Exist?, There's Magic in the Bay...

At the bottom of the stack John found the earliest entry in the collection. Bold letters declared, *Local Fisherman Recounts Run-In with 'Impressive Beast.'* John gawped at their similarity to the words he'd used in his own headline, and as he scanned the story further, there between the columns of text was a photograph of a younger Winslow Hoffner.

John's eyes lit up in shock. He rummaged for earlier issues, but couldn't find any. "Are there more?"

Milly shook her head. "No."

John stood up, pacing and thinking aloud, "There has to be something… When did all the reports begin?"

"Right there on that day," she pointed to the last paper.

"Winslow was even seeing them back then?"

"He's been seeing 'em *everywhere* he goes. He's got the charm, you see — wherever he is."

John stopped in the middle of the floor, surrounded by historic findings and artifacts that proved the existence of mythical creatures, and nearly all of them were hand-delivered by Winslow Hoffner.

Milly looked suddenly concerned. "You believe it all, don't you?"

John broke his trance. "Oh. Yes, of course," he clarified, pushing his fingers through his coppery-brown hair, as the great eye of Gambo flashed through his memory. "*I've experienced too much not to at this point...*" John blinked. "It's just..." He gaped at the nautical treasures around him. "How does *one man* find all this?"

Milly shook her head. "He didn't find them, John. *They* found *him.*"

"Okay..." John tilted his head in thought. "And what does that mean, exactly?"

"It means," Milly took his shoulders, her moon-colored eyes twinkling, "there *weren't* any monsters in Bayfield till Winslow Hoffner came to town."

It Weren't No Sandbar

arm, herby steam piped from John Chaplain's cup of freshly-steeped tea.

"Thank you," he murmured, as he took a long swig and covered his pounding forehead. The ache started to melt as soon as he swallowed.

"Of course, dearie." Milly Matterhorn's shell-strewn jewelry clattered as she lowered into a chair beside him. "You know, I get headaches too every now and then. They say the storms can cause it— changin' pressures and all that."

"Mm-hm."

"Though I suppose finding out monsters are real and pretty much everywhere can cause it too."

John laughed. As he drank down the last of his beverage, he took out his pen and pad and went ahead with the interview, finding out all about animals not yet known to science, which Milly called *cryptids*, along with Bayfield's unusual string of sightings.

"Would it be alright if we took some pictures of the back room?"

"Of course. Are you sure you don't want one of the Squid-Shark first?"

She held up the mangled taxidermy.

John chuckled with her. He took out his company-issued camera and snapped one picture of her posing with the fake animal, then proceeded to the true exhibits, where she carefully extracted one of the artifacts from its glass case.

"Here we are. Perfect." She exhumed something monstrous. "This one was plucked straight outta the bay!"

John froze. Even in the camera's viewfinder, the object was massive: a giant, sand-colored spike, spackled with calcium buildup and dotted by barnacles.

Milly cradled it like an infant and beamed, "Cheese!"

After the flash went off, John lowered his camera to look on the marvel with his own eyes. "Is that a tooth?"

Milly giggled and shook her head. "I ain't hawkin' dinosaurs, dearie."

"A claw?"

"Gettin' *warmer*..."

John stroked his chin in fascination, shaking his head. "I give up. What is it?"

"It's a part of a leg, believe it or not."

"A *leg*?"

Milly nodded.

"From what?"

"Oh, yeah. Biggest lobster ya've ever seen, Keel. This beastie was the *daddy* of all crawdaddies."

Ken Keeley pinched the space between his eyes and sighed. "I can't believe I'm about to humor ye with a question..."

Winslow slurped some root beer, awaiting the moment Ken caved to his curiosity. A tickled laugh slipped through his teeth. "Go 'head, Keeley, y'know ya want to."

"Fine." The cook crossed his arms and slid his toothpick to the corner of his mouth. "How big was it?"

"Big 'nough fer me n' Hank ta mistake its shell fer a sandbar."

A clamor of excited voices and gasps filled every corner of Keeley's Bayside Eatery, as patrons flooded the floors and leaned in to listen. It was the biggest turnout the restaurant had seen in years, and the biggest audience the storyteller had ever had.

Ken chewed his toothpick.

Winslow smiled at him impishly.

"A sandbar."

"Aye."

"How?"

"I was standin' on it."

The crowd exchanged awestruck looks. Their fishstick appetizers went untouched.

"*Standin'* on it?!"

"Aye."

"Why?"

" 'Cause I *thought* it was a sandbar!"

The entranceway cracked. Cold air whistled through the door as Peter Matterhorn shuffled into the packed restaurant. His clouds of breath dissipated in the indoor heat. He unzipped his jacket and pulled off his near-frozen gloves, then took a bewildered look around. It seemed all of Bayfield shared the same craving for fish and beer he did. He navigated the maze of bodies, then realized the source of their fascination.

"It wasn't like I was out there fer no reason, Keel. One o' me outriggers had snagged on a rock. Or so I thought..." Winslow took a long, refreshing sip and smacked his gums. "So we dropped anchor and dinghy'd out ta have a look on this odd lookin' sandbar nearby. Needless ta say, there weren't no rock. And it weren't no sandbar."

"I get it, Wins. I nary believed ye the first time ye said it."

"Nary, eh? Makes perfect sense t'me."

Ken refilled Winslow's root beer, challenging, "O'course it makes sense to *you*. Yer the one makin' it up!"

Winslow angled his eye at the cook. "Consider fer a moment where we is in the world... On record the biggest lobster ever caught was scooped up not far from these waters in 1977."

The audience was enthralled. Some of the younger listeners did internet searches in their phones to validate Winslow's claim.

"He's right!" one teen called.

Ken grumbled.

Winslow pointed at him. "Ha!"

"That ain't proof! That's coincidence."

"That's nature," Winslow rebutted, shrugging. "Bigger a beast is, the more it can eat. The more it can eat, the bigger it gets. Afore long, ya gots yerself a real monster." He winked. "And a darn good story, too."

Peter smiled at the familiar tale as he saddled up at the bar. Muirin scooted through the dense crowd promptly after and poured him a glass of water. He ordered the usual fish and chips and picked a brew listed at the top of their seasonal options, then settled back in his seat and listened.

"I s'pose I knew somethin' was wrong when the thing started ta move. That ain't normal. O'course, from me n' Hank's perspective, we was the ones stayin' put n' our boat was the one floatin' off!

"Naturally, I started hollerin' ta get our third crewman's attention. He was fresh ta the bay, y'see—an ol' pal o' mine visitin' from afar—n' he certainly weren't no sailor. Figured he musta bumped inta the controls or somethin', so I started givin' him a hard time, shoutin'..." Winslow cupped his hands around his mouth. " 'Santiano! Where're ya floatin' off to? How hard is it ta not go nowhere?!'

"And he looked all flustered, n' shouted back, '*You're* the ones who's floatin' away, pendejos!'

"N' I shouted, 'No we ain't!'

"N' he shouted, 'Look down!'

"Then me n' Hank finally looked down n' saw the whole sandbar was shakin' n' gurglin'.

"Santiano shouts, 'I told ya!'

"N' I reply, 'I admit, ya might be onta something...' "

Winslow's audience chuckled. Everyone in the restaurant had grouped up in a tight ring around the storyteller. Their eyes were wide and glittering, excited smiles glued to their features. Even Ken had paused his skepticism to fry up some new orders in the kitchen, and Peter, who was already

67

very familiar with the tale, found himself wrapped up in the magic as well, munching on fish and chips like popcorn at a movie. He had an added curiosity in how the others would react also. Knowing what happened next, he sipped some beer and watched the crowd.

They all jumped when Winslow shot out of his chair. "FOOM! Off we went! Me n' Hank clingin' fer dear life. N' our poor dinghy—*hoh!*—that li'l boat blew ta splinters when this lobby's tail flipped up. The water foamed white, splashin' over the beastie's back ta expose segments o' shell and then—!" Winslow clapped his hands. "Down went Hank."

Everyone gasped.

"Yep. When that beastie got goin' Hank was walloped by its big ol'…" He snapped his fingers, trying to think of the word. "Big ol'…"

"Claw?" someone suggested.

"Thankfully not. *Claws* is what we nicknamed the critter later but not what was swingin' fer Hank at the time…" He wiggled his fingers near his forehead. "These things."

"Antenna?" Ken called from the kitchen.

"Naw."

Sleepy lifted his head from the counter. "Antenn*ae*?"

"Aye, that's it."

Ken cursed. Muirin whapped him.

Winslow went on, "Them whiskers broke the froth when the lobby got up ta speed and came swingin' right fer us like whips. Clocked Hank in the gut real good. Poor fella was shell-shocked."

Sleepy raised his glass. "*Shell!* Ha!"

"Aye, Sleepy." Winslow raised his root beer to cheers him. They toasted, sipped, and Sleepy's head thumped back to the counter. As Winslow wiped soda bubbles from his beard he noticed Peter across the bar. "Matterhorn! Good ta see ya."

"Pleasure's all mine, friend."

Winslow introduced him to the crowd. "This fella runs a great li'l museum with his wife. It's right at the intersection of Barnum n' Shaw, ya can't miss it. Take a trip sometime, ask ta see the back room." He turned back to Peter. "Yer just in time fer the best part, too!" He leaned in to whisper. "No spoilers, aye?"

69

"Wouldn't dream of it."

"Good man!" Winslow clapped his hands, then launched right back into his tale. "Salt n' waves was flyin'. Santiano was far from sight. N' there I was: one hand grippin' the lobby's shell, the other hand grippin' Hank's wrist—and Hank ain't a small human, neither. I can hardly keep the man upright after he's thoroughly examined a bottle o' whiskey, keep in mind. Whenever the beast's tail flapped, my friend went flappin' as well. Felt like I was holdin' a flounder by the tail. Then, the most amazin' thing came inta view…"

Keeley returned from the kitchen, wiping his hands with a cloth. "A camera crew to document the evidence?"

"Naw. Better! A cave." Winslow rose from his seat, his fingers moving mystically and massive right eye shimmering as he swept the audience. "Bright blue in color, spackled with barnacles n' coral, and inside, somethin' was glowin'…"

Winslow set one foot back on his barstool and one elbow on the counter. " 'Course I had no idea just how amazin' it was at the time. I was more concerned with the sandbar-sized lobster barrelin'

70

toward these sharp rocks at full-speed." The fisherman got low. "I curled up best I could with the space I had, bracin' fer impact 'cause this ride wasn't slowin'. But at the last second, the beastie flipped around a hundred-eighty degrees, buckin' us inta the cave while its hindquarters plugged up the exit.

"Hank n' me musta traded consciousness after we landed, 'cause I woke up ta this ringin' in me ears, n' my first mate was up n' about, cheerin', 'Wins, Wins, get up ye coot, have a look a' this!' The cave was full o' gold."

Peter smiled at the crowd's amazed reaction. They flooded him with questions:

"What kind of gold?" someone asked.

"Coins, mostly," Winslow said. "Some type o' doubloon. Spanish, I think."

"Were they real?"

"Real 'nough ta turn Hank's eyes inta saucers. He was fillin' every pocket."

"How many did you grab?" Keeley queried.

"Two or three."

"Be real, Wins."

"I am."

"Yer tellin' me ye didn't take the whole cave-full? What fella comes 'cross treasure like that to just pass it up?"

"I'd just rodeoed a prehistoric lobster, Keel! What use was doubloons ta me? 'Sides, most treasures ain't gold, anyhow."

Ken crossed his arms.

Winslow continued, "My only worry was gettin' back ta me boat. N' at the time, that seemed darn near impossible. The only exit was blocked by a big, flippin' lobster tail. Filled up the whole space nearly; we was trapped. I remember Hank standin' next ta me, wearin' some crown he found. 'We're gonna be here a while,' he said.

"*Eye Spy* got old fairly quick when alls ya gots is treasure n' stone. Hank ended up talkin' most the night about what he wanted ta buy when he traded in the gold. Said he'd get a submarine one day." Winslow chuckled. "I said I'd get a case o' root beer."

The audience laughed. Keeley refilled his glass.

"When mornin' came, n' we saw the beast's back legs n' tail was still there, we knew we wasn't gettin' outta there if we didn't think smartly. The lobby was lookin' real still, so Hank thought it might be nappin'. We got up close n' gave it a poke. Nothin'. There was one big leg blockin' our way now, so Hank n' me tried ta lift it..."

Winslow made a popping sound. "I'd hardly touched the thing and its foot popped off!" He winked at Peter. "You know what that's like, eh?"

Peter laughed.

"At first I was horrified, but then I realized how light it was. What I was holdin' was hollow. What was left standin' in the cave was too. A great big, empty shell. The lobby had molted!"

The audience erupted with thrilled laughter and more questions:

"How did you get back?"

"Santiano eventually found us. We could tell it was him 'cause he had the boat goin' one knot n' was fishtailin' all over. Had ta shout directions at him on how ta stop afore he hit the shore."

"Where did the lobster go?" one woman asked.

"Back ta the bay, I s'pose. I'm guessin' it was just lookin' fer a safe place ta shed fer the night. Cave was the perfect spot. When we floated back ta harbor we didn't see no trace o' her." Winslow gulped down the last of his drink. "N' you know what that means..."

Keeley grinned knowingly. "What's that, Wins?"

"Means the beastie's still out there, n' *bigger* this time!"

The whole restaurant erupted with applause. It took Winslow by surprise. Peter finished his beer and clapped along. Keeley gazed out at the cheering throng and set his elbow down near Winslow. "Looks like ye could spin these tales fer a livin', huh?"

"N' leave the bay? Where'd I get all me best stories then?" Winslow slapped Ken's arm.

Ken laughed. "Ye seem to have an endless supply. I nearly forgot I didn't believe ye this time."

Winslow squinted at him. "Ya laugh now, but I tells ya, I couldn't eat lobster fer *years* after that."

"That's 'cause ye couldn't afford it."

Winslow smirked. "Yeah, p'rhaps yer right, Keel." He reached into his shirt pocket and took out an antiquated, gold doubloon. He held it to the light and the restaurant went quiet with awe when their eyes caught its shine. Winslow flipped the coin Ken's way. "Everyone's meal is on me tonight, by the way."

Winslow made his exit. Everyone scrambled to look over the counter at the treasure in Keeley's hands. The cook held it over his head and shouted at the fisherman, "Do ye make these trinkets ahead o' time?!"

Outside, Peter caught up with him. "That story's one of my favorites."

"Thanks, Matterhorn. Happy ya stopped by. How's the Countess?"

Peter grinned. "Doing well. She's over at the museum chattin' with that reporter from the Messenger."

"Chaplain?"

"Yep. He's interviewing her for another story."

Winslow walked at his side. "Well maybe I'll drops by n' say hi then. Yer lady still makin' that famous tea?"

Peter laughed and started to answer, when a third man shuffled through the cold. Clouds puffed from his mouth as he called, "*Wins!*"

"What's the matter, Hank? Ya look like ya've seen a—"

"There's somethin' out there!"

"What?"

"Somethin' in the bay. Somethin' big."

Snowflakes twirled by as Peter looked to each of the fishermen, a blend of terror and wonder on his face.

Winslow stepped forward. "How big're we talkin'?"

"Wins," Hank panted. "The growl she made shook the boat!"

Albert Nguyen flipped through the draft of John's new story, smiling as he reached the picture of Milly holding the monstrous leg-shell.

"Fabulous," he said. A smile wrinkled his kind old face, as he tapped the pages into a neat stack and set them on the corner of his desk. He stifled a cough and stood. "Well done, John. Our readers will love it. Keep writing like this and we'll have to give you your very own column."

"Wow, really?"

"Absolutely." Albert paced over to his office's window which overlooked a town alit by yellow squares spackling every building. Beyond them, the lapping waves of the bay were painted the same nighttime tones, as a beam flashed from a far-off lighthouse to decorate its crests with wriggling, golden bands.

A mix of rain and snow was coming down, slithering over the glass just as it had during John's first interview with Winslow.

John thanked his editor-in-chief for the compliments, staring over his shoulder at the intensifying storm, then refocusing on his own reflection in the distorting, mirror-like surface.

"You know," Albert said, removing his glasses and rubbing his eyes. "I actually remember those old news stories you referenced. I used to read them back in the day. Every breakfast I'd see what new monster had cropped up in the bay." Albert shook his head at the fond memory, running fingers over his grayed sideburns. "Suddenly, though, the news diluted. Local became global, sensationalism wasn't sensational enough, and the same generic stories ran week after week..."

The lighthouse made a rotation, flashing, and a rumble came from the clouds.

"I'm glad you're writing for us, John. You remind me a lot of myself when I first started out. I knew a good story when I heard one."

John grinned proudly. "Thank you, Mr. Nguyen."

"Call me Albert."

"Thank you, Albert."

The editor-in-chief nodded, clasped his hands behind his back, and watched the town. John looked over his boss' shoulder at the reflection of himself again. This time it aligned with the lighthouse.

"I suspect you've joined our team at the perfect time, John," Albert added, as the lighthouse's beam swept over the bay. "Perhaps this town is ready to embrace its strange history yet again."

Midnight on the Seanna

loorboards creaked. Wallboards groaned. A bell clanged outside as cranky gales swirled into the harbor, battering fishing vessels with rain, wind, and sleet, as frantic captains hollered and rushed to keep their boats aground. All but Winslow Hoffner, who stood silently in the lower deck of the Seanna, which, like her captain, seemed unimpressed by the sky's sudden tantrum.

On a sheltered section of the main deck, first mate Hank Malloy lounged dozily in a flat chair that was so repaired and re-repaired, its cushions were mostly duct tape. They stuck to his faded blue overalls as he shifted forward to glimpse the tempest's mutating clouds. In one hand, his fingers drummed an old, wooden fishing net. He frowned at the sky.

"C'mon now, stormy. Whot'cha got?"

The skies replied with a distant rumble.

"*Pfft.* Class one at best..." Hank grumbled, dissatisfied. He gulped some whiskey and resumed taunting, "Let it out! Where's yer lungs?"

A deeper boom thundered.

Hank paled. "Gettin' there." He shifted to call down the ladders. "Ey, Wins! Have ye found it yet?"

The first mate's calls echoed apart on their way to Winslow's ears. The fisherman blinked and rubbed his knee, then shuffled over to his messy desk where a drawer had fallen open.

Sapphire flashed through the boat as lightning cracked the sky.

"*That's* what I'm talkin' about!" Hank cheered.

As the space dimmed and Winslow squinted to adjust his vision, his hand ventured onward to explore the drawer's cluttered contents. Somewhere amid the darkness his fingertips grasped it and brought it to his sight: an old, tanned photograph, edges frayed, image spotted. Beyond the spots of age and dust stood three proud men. The first, himself. Skinny as ever, but fit. On

82

the other side, Hank. Rotund and happy, barrel-chested. Even then, he sported the same unruly red mutton chops, which framed a wide, cheery mouth gaped in mid-laugh. And between the pair, a tall, sturdy figure dressed in black. Bald, with a prominent nose and serious, dark eyes.

Winslow brought the picture closer and sighed. Though the middle figure's eyes were dour, the faintest trace of humor was still alive in his smile, tugged to one side, almost invisibly. In one black-gloved hand, he gripped the jaw of a smallmouth bass that looked no bigger than the lure he used to catch it. In the other, he displayed a trophy far more impressive than his catch.

Winslow chuckled softly, then flipped the photo over. On the back he spotted a single, faded word scribbled in pencil: *Churubusco.*

Winslow's throat knotted, and he dropped it. The photo sheened in blue glow before twisting and settling like a fall leaf on the table. Thunder trailed its lightning and rattled the Seanna's walls as rain pelted harder. From this new angle the middle figure's smile had vanished completely.

Winslow stood back, eyes locked with the man in the photo. Before long, its sepia tones seemed to bleed and drift outward, painting a memory framed by plots of wild, rustling wheat. The storm intensified, pattering the porthole just as it had pattered the windshield of a 1955 pickup. Thunder shuddered the walls and joggled the floors, and Winslow felt himself bounce and land in an upholstered passenger seat.

The Indiana farmland blurred outside the blotted window, as their rickety red truck puttered down the uneven country road.

"What are you drawing there?" the man in the driver's seat asked.

Winslow didn't respond. He dragged a chewed-up pencil along the cream paper of a small, leather-bound sketchbook to make an outline.

After a moment of awkward silence, the driver cleared his throat and went on, "I have a good feeling about tonight's expedition."

"Mm-hm."

"The reports of this creature are..." the driver rubbed his chin with one of his black-gloved hands, "fascinating. If they're true they'll definitely give

Canvey Island a run for its money." He chuckled lightly. "What do you think?"

"Mm-hm."

"Alright, clearly you're preoccupied."

"What was that?"

The driver sighed. "I think we're almost there." His dark eyes glanced at the navigational device he'd clipped to the dashboard, a brass-colored, compass-looking instrument. "What did you think of the briefing?"

"Didn't think much of it."

"So, you didn't read it."

"Yep."

"*'Yep* you read it, or *yep* it went unread?"

"You got it, Scialpi."

Giuseppe Scialpi let out a long breath of aggravation through his nose, as one hand strayed from the wheel to massage his right temple. He then dropped a stack of papers overtop Winslow's drawing.

"Hey—!"

"Why don't you take a crash-course?"

Winslow slipped his pencil behind his ear and cracked the topmost folder. In red ink,

CLASSIFIED was stamped across its front beside a small, circular icon that resembled the planet Saturn. The next few pages were nondisclosure notices. Winslow scoffed at the formality. "Why all the legal decoration?"

"Just read the thing, Winslow."

He finally reached the biographical section of the alleged monster and read, *"Beast of Busco,"* under his breath before muttering the rest.

The truck hit a bump.

"Would ya watch how yer drivin' this time-capsule? I'm tryin' ta read."

"Don't blame me for the conditions of your cram-session."

Winslow squinted into the document, then asked, "So it's a big snappin' turtle?"

"Supposedly."

Winslow read on. *"Last official measurements... four feet 'cross the shell... five-hundred pounds —* Good grief! That's a healthy critter." He flipped ahead to newspaper clippings and looked them over. "These reports are over twenty years old, Scialpi."

"Indeed they are."

"If he's still kickin' about, this Busco Beastie's gonna be way bigger now…" Winslow flipped to archived reports in the file that detailed varying measurements, sample reports, and shell types. "Or there may be others. What're the suits askin' us ta do when we spot 'im?"

"Standard protocol."

"Tracker goin' out?"

Scialpi nodded. "It is."

"Alrighty. The ol' switcheroo then." Winslow leaned back. "Fair 'nough." He set the documents aside in exchange for his sketchbook.

Scialpi chanced a peek at his friend's drawing. Winslow was shading in the fur of an elegant, seal-like creature. He nodded, his eyes gliding back to the road. "How's Anna doing, by the way?"

"Fine." Winslow added detail and shine to the creature's eyes.

"That's good to hear. I know for a while there… Did you ever figure out why—"

The scratching of Winslow's pencil grew louder as he added in a background.

Scialpi cleared his throat. "Do you not want to talk about it?"

"Just drive, Scialpi."

The red pickup rumbled and turned off onto a darker, narrower dirt road, where Scialpi pulled over and parked. He squinted through the rain-distorted headlight beam at the empty, muddy path, then checked his navigational tool. Its needle rotated forward, quivered, then spun backward.

"No... Can't be right..." Scialpi murmured.

Still sketching, Winslow commented, "That thing's a hunk o' junk, Scialpi."

"It was working just fine on the way here."

"Yeah, and now it ain't. The thing goes caput soon as it gets anywhere close ta somethin' worth seein'. Which means ol' Busco's somewhere nearby."

"Oh, *flawless* logic," Scialpi said, running his gloved hand over his scalp. "Perhaps I made a wrong turn."

"Wrong turn ta the right place."

Scialpi frowned and shook the instrument. Its needle rattled.

Winslow closed his sketchbook, looping a leather ribbon around a button on its cover to fasten it shut. "Weren't ya hearin' me? The one thing ya can count on a Cryptolabe ta do is break at the worst possible time." Winslow rolled down his passenger side window and sniffed the damp air. He nodded at a smell. "Oh, yeah. This is the spot."

"Oh, really?" Scialpi scowled. "Do you have a new power now? Some heightened sense of smell I'm unaware of?"

Winslow opened the door to step out, but Scialpi pulled him back inside by the elbow. "Where are you going?"

"This is the spot, Scialpi."

"We don't *know* that."

Winslow looked offended. "Speak fer yerself! Isn't this why ya brought me out here in the first place? *Begged* me ta transfer? Ya said it yerself in that letter o' yers. Said I'd be yer 'charm' or whatever."

Scialpi's eyes cooled. "I did." He took a few, slow, shaky breaths. "No doubt," he admitted. "Unusual things tend to happen when you're around."

"Then what's the matter?"

Scialpi shook his head. "Even if this *was* the place, you're unprepared. Where's your..." His next question was answered when he found a black jacket crumpled up at his friend's feet. He picked it up and flattened out the wrinkles. "Are you *kidding* me?"

"I ain't wearin' that."

"This is the uniform, Winslow, you have to."

"Why?"

"Because *those* are the rules." Scialpi pushed it into his hands. "If for some reason other agents were to get involved you'd want them to know you're with us."

"They know who I am," Winslow grumbled as he unfolded the black fabric. He cringed at the sight of it. "Hate this thing. Hate this patch." He pointed to the right sleeve's yellow, shield-shaped patch that was festooned with the black Saturn insignia. "Makes us look like we're chasin' aliens or somethin'."

Scialpi shrugged and fiddled with his Cryptolabe.

"Hey, the suits ain't chasin' aliens, right?"

"No," Scialpi said, returning to his work. He looked up again, a thoughtful expression on his face. "Not as far as *my* clearance goes, anyway."

The rain pattered harder. Winslow pulled on his jacket. "I ain't chasin' aliens…"

The Cryptolabe finally reactivated. It made a lively hum as the small meter bulbs on its outer ring blinked and its needle swiveled back to the main road.

"Ah-ha! There we go. We're back in business." Scialpi shifted the truck out of park.

"Scialpi, I'm tellin' ya, we're already here—"

"I have a strong reading coming from the north; this isn't it."

"Ya've got a strong *lie* comin' from the north; this *is* it."

"I know you don't trust *science*, Winslow, but seeing as you're not the one helming this investigation at the moment, I suggest—"

"I trust science plenty, Scialpi, but what we're dealin' with ain't science—!"

A sonorous, bugling tone vibrated ahead of them as a large, black blur stomped across the road. The two halted their altercation to watch in awe as a mammoth, shelled monster passed through the truck's headlights and plodded into the woods, trees falling in its wake. Winslow and Scialpi's

91

heads slowly rotated to one another. The Cryptolabe's needle made a mousey squeak and twisted south.

"Told ya," Winslow said.

The two scrambled out of the car. Winslow took off at the lead with his friend frantically filling a bag with supplies.

"C'mon, Scialpi. All ya need's the trank n' the new tracker."

"I'm coming." A load of equipment, much of which Winslow deemed unnecessary, jostled in a duffle bag as Scialpi ran. Winslow rolled his eyes and sprinted on.

They burst into the thicket. Branches snapped and loose leaves fluttered past as they followed the muddy, sunken trail of the giant beast, framed by fractured trees.

"How can a turtle be so fast?" Scialpi puffed.

"Ain't tough ta outrun a man carryin' a whole laboratory on his back."

Scialpi growled under his breath, then gawped ahead. In the distance, a large tree fell. He panted, "This thing's more dangerous than I anticipated."

"He's just spooked."

"That doesn't matter if—" Another tree trunk cleaved apart. A flock of crows cawed and scattered from its falling branches. "—being spooked means taking down a whole forest!" The two chased on.

Eventually, the trees stopped falling. Winslow and Scialpi jogged through a large, broken archway in the trunks that opened to a flat, grassy clearing at the base of a quarry. The rain had settled into a mist that hung over a dark, watery pit at its center, which gurgled a few bubbles, before its rippling surface stilled.

"Damn," Scialpi fumed, dropping his duffle bag and gripping his knees to catch his breath.

Winslow scratched the back of his head. "Ah, well. It was a good chase fer a while there."

Scialpi muttered something angrily and held his head.

"Ain't no big deal."

"It *is*, Winslow, we were hired to—wait, where's your jacket?"

Winslow looked down at his plain, buttoned shirt. "Oh, huh, would ya look at that." He laughed awkwardly. "Musta flown off me in all the excitement."

"Are you joking?"

"I ain't jokin', it was plenty exciting."

"What's *wrong* with you? We'll never get anywhere in this business." Scialpi paced. "This is the type of behavior that'll make us look like reckless, screw-up, loose cannons to the board of directors. They won't stand for it! They won't tolerate it!"

Winslow muttered, "*Someone bought a thesaurus.*"

Scialpi sneered.

Winslow chortled. "Loose cannons." He smiled dreamily at the term. "Gotta admit that sounds pretty cool."

"Dammit, Winslow, listen to me—!"

They broke into an argument, their voices blending into cluttered echoes that ricocheted through the lonely quarry and amplified off the broken rocks and boulders framing its waterhole.

"*Yer* the one that asked *me* ta come here."

"Does that make you free of regulation?"

Winslow shrugged. "It'd be nice ta not be hounded 'bout it all the time."

Scialpi stomped toward the waterhole, clipping Winslow's shoulder as he passed. "I intend to do this by the books." He leaned against one of the quarry's boulders, squinting out over the dark lake. *"Maybe we can set up a perimeter..."*

"We ain't settin' up a perimeter."

Scialpi looked annoyed. "Maybe *you* won't, but I will." He took out a radio and beaconed. A red light blinked.

"Scialpi, it ain't in the water."

"What are you talking about? Of course it's—"

A deep bugling tone made Scialpi jump, as the boulder behind him rumbled and rose up on huge, clawed feet. His shoes lost traction on the slick grass and he flopped onto the ground, as a thick, fleshy neck vibrated another booming call and pushed out an armored, primordial head through the shade of its shell. Scialpi was locked in fear, as the Beast of Busco's wet, hazel eyes gleamed and jagged, grim beak gaped.

Winslow grabbed his pal by the loops of his elbows and pulled hard. The Beast of Busco hissed and chomped at him, clapping on the tail of his black jacket. A huge tear ripped through the fabric as Winslow dragged him to safety and got him to his feet.

"Y'alright?"

Scialpi's eyes were wide. He patted himself down, finding no abrasions, then looked at his arms. Only the sleeves and shoulders of his agency jacket remained. The rest had torn at the seams and was languidly being chewed by the monster.

"Hey!" Scialpi roared.

Winslow held him back. "Ain't worth it, buddy, ain't worth it." The Beast of Busco gulped down what remained of Scialpi's uniform and blinked contentedly.

Scialpi slumped over in disbelief.

Winslow patted his shoulder. "Looks like we're *both* loose cannons now, huh?"

The beast's sickle-sized, bear-like claws scratched the earth as he dragged forward, dwarfing the two men and eclipsing the moonlight. He resembled a dinosaur, nearly eight feet tall at the top of his shell.

"What a monster," Scialpi breathed.

"What a beauty," Winslow commented. He patted his shaken friend's shoulder again and sauntered toward the beast.

Scialpi went to grab him but missed. *"What are you doing?"* he whispered harshly.

"We got ourselves a job, 'member?" Winslow winked. "I got this, Scialpi, don't worry."

Scialpi shivered as he watched Winslow stride before the immense creature. His friend puffed out his chest, keeping his eye angled at the great turtle, who huffed and bugled as he sculled to a halt in the gravel before him, nostrils flaring and blowing back Winslow's ash blond hair.

"Easy there, beastie." Winslow held out his hand peacefully and whispered, *"Yer a fighter. That's how ya scraped by so long. I respect that."*

The Beast of Busco growled a reply.

Winslow bent his knees. Keeping one hand raised while his other ventured to retrieve Scialpi's duffle bag, he continued soothing the beast, *"Just know I ain't gonna hurt ya."* He snatched up the heavy equipment.

Scialpi swallowed nervously, as he watched his friend sort through the mess of gizmos to find the tranquilizer and the new tracker, then froze when he set the tranquilizer back inside.

"What're you doing?" Scialpi hissed.

Winslow whispered back, "See his size? Not 'nough juice in one dart. Two darts is too many."

"Just give him one, then. Get him tired."

"Naw."

"What do you mean, 'naw'?"

"I ain't doin' it. He's too old fer it. Plus we're gettin' close ta construction sites now, n' I don't want 'im spotted afore sunup. Can't have a drunken cryptid hobblin' through the streets. Now hush up a moment..."

Scialpi's heart thudded.

Winslow took out a gadget and activated the switch. A green light blinked. "No worries, beastie, just givin' ya a new accessory..."

The monster thrummed a calm note. Winslow eased further and patted its head, chuckling, while Scialpi looked on in utter disbelief.

"I see yer game, now. Yer too big ta be bothered by anythin', ain't ya?"

The beast bugled musically.

"Thought so."

Winslow kept eye contact with the beast as he knelt to find the old tracker fastened to a spiky shell outgrowth and replace it. He tugged on the release mechanism, which was gnarled with a tangle of knotted, muddy weeds. *"Dagnab..."*

"Hurry, Winslow."

The Beast of Busco's beak parted with a dreary howl.

"Winslow!"

"I got it, Scialpi, calm down."

A popping crack split the night like thunder. Winslow ducked down to clutch his ringing ears, then flinched when something cold touched his skin. The old tracker lay in his palms amid a pool of dark blood.

"Scialpi..." Winslow uttered, though he couldn't hear his own voice. Through the mist he saw his friend, a revolver in his hands, smoke snaking from the barrel. *"What did ya...?"*

A distorted, distant-sounding wail shattered his focus: the maimed, mangled bugle of the Beast of Busco. It shrilled and reeled at a spewing wound in its neck.

"What did ya do?" Winslow could hear himself now. "Scialpi, what'd ya do?!"

Scialpi looked panicked, as the bloodied monster came barreling toward him. He unloaded his gun, one more round finding the flesh on its neck, while the rest sparked off its shell.

Scialpi was plowed over and his leg crunched sideways under the beast's weight. His sharp outcry mimicked the creature's as he sprawled out to the side and the Beast of Busco stamped out of view, howling. Scialpi touched his twisted leg and winced, then tried to stand. Winslow tackled him.

"Why'd ya do it?!" he shrieked, clawing him by the collar and slamming him twice. "Y'said standard protocol!"

"It *is* protocol!" Scialpi shoved him. "The animal's unhinged and unsafe."

"Ya say the same things 'bout me! Why don't ya shoot me too, then?!"

Scialpi scowled. "Gun's empty."

Black helicopters chopped the clouds, their red lights matching the beacon on Scialpi's radio. Winslow grimaced and chucked the device in the water. He shuddered as if struck by freeze. "*We*

100

gotta fix this..." he uttered. He wiped his eye and turned to his friend. "Scialpi, we gotta —" Scialpi was gone. He spun to look for him, then heard another bugle coming from the right and sprinted.

Around a stack of cleaved rocks Winslow found both of them limping.

"Scialpi!" he called.

The Beast of Busco whimpered, trailing blood. Scialpi shambled, stone in hand.

"Don't!"

The sharp rock came down on the animal's skull with a spattering crack. The heavy shell dropped to the mud, and Winslow dropped to his knees.

Around him, helicopters made improvised landings and men in dark coats came filing out, seemingly absent of sound. One group tended to Scialpi's leg while another secured hooks around the brim of the cryptid's shell. Before long, he watched the body lift from sight by helicopter, and his sense of hearing snapped back with the sharp squeak of the pickup's straining flatbed.

A hand touched Winslow's shoulder and he shot up, fists balled, lunging.

"Whoa, whoa, calm down!" one of the suited men implored.

Winslow huffed as his eyes lifted from the black Saturn logo to the agent's face. He recognized him. Carlos Santiano.

"It's alright, pal, keep cool."

Winslow pushed away from him.

"Giuseppe looks like he took a hit," Santiano commented, gesturing toward Scialpi, whose leg was being wrapped in a compression bandage. "Looks like we showed up in the nick of time."

"Yeah." Winslow marched after his partner. "Might wanna get another set o' bandages ready…"

"Yes, yes, I'm fine, really," Scialpi said to the medics. "A water would be great, thank—"

Winslow punched him in the jaw. "Sorry, Scialpi! Standard protocol!" The bandaged man toppled backward as agents rushed in to separate them.

Scialpi's gloved hand wiped his mouth and his dark eyes rose to Winslow's, as an ocean of suited bodies swept them apart.

Santiano chased after his restrained friend. Winslow was squirming in the arms of the other agents, yelling at them to let him go.

"I'll watch him," Santiano said, breaking up the chaos, then ordered the agents to tend to Scialpi, taking Winslow by the wrist. The agents dispersed. Winslow's lip twitched. His eyes were downcast. Santiano cupped his shoulder. "What happened? Why'd you attack him?"

"He didn't have ta..." Winslow started. "The critter... it was docile, he didn't have ta..."

"Take a breath."

Winslow shut his eyes, head shaking. "The sound it made..." He shot alert again when an engine started across the woods. He took off running.

"Winslow!"

Feeling outside his body, Winslow took off, weaving around trunks, ducking under branches. A clamor of footsteps and frenzied voices trailed in his wake. On a tree stump, he found the black coat he'd discarded and pulled it on.

A dark-haired agent completed a careful Y-turn to pivot the old pickup in the correct direction. The vehicle moved sluggishly with the Beast of Busco's heavy body loaded in the back. Winslow ran out in front of the truck, waving his arms. It stopped. He gave the driver a thumbs-up, then went up to the truck's window and knocked.

The agent rolled down the glass. "What's going on?"

"Ya forgot somethin'."

He frowned in perplexity. "What?"

A fist to the face promptly dizzied him, and Winslow pulled him from the truck. Reading his nametag, he apologized, "Sorry, Shore," then hopped in the driver's seat. He pulled off his agency jacket and went to pull the door closed, but a hand caught it.

Santiano pleaded, "Winslow, stop this. Get out of the truck. If you feel something unprofessional happened then let me hear your side. We can all sit down and discuss it."

"Wouldn't have happened…"

"What?"

"If I hadn't been here…" Winslow's voice shook. "He used me…"

Santiano wasn't making sense of his words. "We can talk about it at HQ when we write up the report—"

Winslow tugged on the door again, but Santiano held it open.

"We'll figure it out, Winslow. Just please—"

Winslow's eyes struck him. They were flooding over with tears. "Santiano, move."

Santiano felt his grip loosen. The door slammed shut, and the truck rumbled down the dirt road, drenching the other pursing agents as he ran over a puddle and sped off.

With the beast's body in tow, Winslow headed north. He wiped his eyes as the sky opened up again, the red pickup was quaked with thundering laments, and the needle of the Cryptolabe was sent into a wild spiral.

Another powerful strike vibrated the steel, then another. The vehicle rattled; joggling, bouncing, and landing Winslow back on the creaking wooden floorboards of the Seanna.

He blinked and wiped his eyes on his sleeve, then saw the picture of him, Hank, and Scialpi. He caught himself slipping it into an old photo frame.

A thunderous boom rattled his wall of photos, pictures, and art.

"Woo-hoo! Wins, did ye feel that'n?" Hank cheered.

Winslow didn't answer. The acrylic seagull he took from Keeley's eyed him curiously from beside the framed front page of the Bayfield Messenger's latest issue.

When the sky thundered again, Hank piped up once more, "Did ye find it yet? How long ye been down there?" Winslow could hear Hank shifting, trying to get out of the reclined chair as its duct-taped cushions made sputtering, ripping sounds. "Ye'd better say somethin' soon, or I'm comin' tae get ye, chair adhered!"

"Comin'," Winslow managed to answer. The photo lay in a clutter of sundries in his desk drawer. He shut it.

Hank swiveled stiffly as Winslow ascended the ladders and pulled up a chair. "*There* ye are!" Hank waved his fishing net like a flag. "I don't even remember what I asked ye tae get!"

Winslow revealed his old sketchbook, leather binds peeling, stitching frayed. On the cover was a faded wooden plaque with an etched title: *Journal of Curiosities.*

Hank's eyes flashed. "Aye, now I remember."

Winslow took a seat and flipped through the blotted, old pages. Messy ink scribblings of monsters and notes flickered by. From a cooler he took out a can of root beer and cracked it with his free hand, then tapped drinks with his friend.

"Have ya heard the right kind yet?"

Hank shook his head, disappointed. "Storm's not cooperatin'."

A bassy, bellowing tone pulsed from above.

"How 'bout that?"

"Not quite." Hank downed his drink and waved his net like a maestro's baton. "Sing fer me stormy, sing!"

Winslow put his hand over Hank's net and lowered it from the crackling sky. "Prolly not a good idea."

"Oh, yeah. Very true."

The two laughed, then hushed when a deeper boom with a different quality was heard. It struck nearby, crashing with such power and ferocity, the whole boat shook beneath them, before it lilted and groaned with a final, trebling hum. The water itself seemed to still, foam popping, before the waves resumed.

"*That's* it." Hank's eyes met with Winslow's. "*That's* what I heard — what she sounded like!"

The distant thunders that followed seemed embarrassed and outdone. Hank noticed he was gripping his net close to his chest. He glimpsed its measly weave, then chucked it aside, thoroughly spooked.

Winslow, too, was in awe. He flipped more rapidly to the back of his sketchbook, where fewer pictures were drawn and paragraphs of notes dominated the pages. He pointed to one. "Here."

"Class eight..." Hank mumbled as he read, squinting through the dimness, as a sharp, icy breeze swirled in, trying to flip the page over. Winslow held it down with his thumb. Much to Hank's chagrin, the section lacked any of Winslow's trademark drawings.

"That's 'cause I've never seen it," Winslow explained. "No one has." He sipped his soda, then clarified, "Well, not all of it at least. A part o' the beastie washed up way back in 1896, but later on they tried ta pass it off as a decayin' blob o' whale blubber."

"Cover-up, eh?"

"Aye."

"Convenient," Hank grumbled, and continued reading between sips of whiskey. *"The St. Augustine Mystery..."* His eyes grew bigger as he found the biographical write-up. Sleet skittered over the dock's bells to percussion eerie chimes. Hank shivered. "That's the one."

Winslow's eye quivered. He nodded. "Alrighty."

"What do ye think, Wins? Too dangerous?"

Winslow reviewed his notes. No data was logged about the ferocity of the beast. Only speculation with references to legends of similar monsters during the Age of Exploration. Winslow's eye shimmered. He sniffed the moist air, then leaned back in his chair and shrugged. "I seen worse."

Hank's red mutton chops seemed to puff out as a big grin filled his face. "We're back at it, then! Ha-haw!" He pumped a new drink in the air, toasting, *"Slàinte don mhuir!"*

Winslow echoed him and clicked his soda can against the glass. They drank, gazing out at the chaotic twists above and the sloshing, harried currents below.

"Still," Hank admitted, wiping his chin, "an expedition this big 'quires more than just us, don'tcha think? We'd need an extra crewman."

"Yer right," Winslow said. Tilting his sketchbook, a business card from the Bayfield Messenger tumbled from its pages. He lifted the contact to his eye and smiled. "And as luck would have it, I know a guy."

For Yer Eyes Only

ipping envelopes and flattening paper into semi-even stacks, John Chaplain sat alone in the dark, secluded mailroom of the Bayfield Messenger. A single rectangular window hung above him, exaggerating the dungeonous feel of his cramped workspace while silver streaks of moonlight skated over the litter of documents he'd been tasked to organize. So much had changed in a week. He sighed.

A creak on the deformed floor drew his eyes to a familiar silhouette. He smiled. "Hey, Becci."

Becci Hamrin stood in the doorway, the light of an active newsroom gleaming behind her.

"Hey, John." She squinted through the dark. "Why don't you turn the lights on?" She flipped the switch, and the fluorescent bulbs flickered like

113

strobes and crackled like insects on a bug zapper. "Oh." She flipped them off, the lights faded, and John shrugged to his shadowed work station.

"I'm pretty sure this place is haunted."

"I believe you." Becci crossed her arms. Her freckled nose cringed at a musty smell. "I can't believe Nell stuck you down here," she murmured. "I didn't even know this place existed. How are you holding up?"

"Oh, you know," John said. "Only gave myself five papercuts today."

"Nice."

"Mm-hm." He sliced open another envelope. This one was a fan letter from a long-time reader about the Gambo piece. John's expression softened. "It's not all bad, though."

Becci strolled over the groaning floor to join John by his tiny desk. "Yeah, in a space like this you can take up mushroom growing in your spare time."

John chuckled. He filed the fanmail away and cut open another envelope.

Becci took something from her coat pocket. "I know you're probably tired of looking at letters, but…" She handed John a folded, handmade card. "We're all signing it for the boss."

In big, green letters the note read, *Get Well Soon, Albert!* on the front, with the inside decorated by signatures of nearly every journalist at the Messenger scribed in a rainbow of multicolored inks. John drew a pen from his shirt pocket and found a small spot in the corner to add his name.

"Sorry there isn't a lot of space left."

"No worries," John said. "Did you hear what he has?"

"Pneumonia."

John's brow slanted in concern. "Must be this weather." His throat knotted as he signed his name in neat, dark swirls in the bottom right, trying to conserve space. *John Chaplain.* He capped his pen. Above his name he found another, bolder signature that inhabited most of the middle section of the card. A single word: *Nell.*

John grimaced and handed the card back to Becci, suddenly aware of the clamor of clacking keyboards outside. "Thanks for stopping in," John said, keeping his head low to his work.

"Think you'll be free one of these nights to hang out? Get a drink, maybe?"

John's blue eyes rose to meet hers. A smile broke free for a moment on both of their faces. "Yeah." His expression sank again when he glimpsed the massive stack of documents waiting to be organized. "I'll probably need one after I get through all this." He scowled at the papers. *Thanks a lot, Nell.*

"That's the spirit, Johnny," a slick voice cut in.

John froze. As if summoned by his angry thoughts, Nell Dunney appeared, circling his desk. He was wrapped in a gray turtleneck and dark gray slacks. In his teeth he twisted a fresh, cherry lollipop. His coaly eyes examined the mess of letters.

"How's the new job treating you?"

Terrible, John thought. "Fine," he answered. "Almost through the second box."

"Good, good." Nell nudged him. "You know I couldn't trust just *anyone* to work on something this important. Right, Johnny?"

Yeah, you had to torture me specifically. "Right," John said.

116

"With Albert out of commission, I've got a lot to deal with. I appreciate you stepping up to the challenge. Being my right-hand man and all." Nell slapped John's shoulder. "We're on deadline." He glanced at Becci. "Speaking of which, I still need your final draft in the drop folder by tonight, Beck."

"On it."

John watched her slip back to the spectacular chaos of the newsroom, her strawberry hair swaying. He stapled a letter, and set it on a stack of possible story leads. Nell's hand covered the pages.

"I've got another job for you since you're so efficient. Distribute any promising leads to the newsroom for next week's issue."

"Alright," John said, filing through his memory for what story he'd most want to write.

Nell made a knowing grin. "And remember, you aren't writing this week. I need your help with the editing."

John went rigid. He picked up another letter.

"Don't look so down, Johnny. I know you'd rather be out on the docks somewhere listening to geriatrics ramble on about fish, but look at it this way—"

John frowned. His letter opener made a jagged tear.

"I'm broadening your work experience. A journalist of your caliber shouldn't be pigeonholed, Johnny. I want to make *full* use of your talents. I'm liberating you." He opened his arms, his hands nearly touching either wall.

"*Ow!*" John shook his hand. Nell was quick to provide a tissue, but John waved it away, holding his sixth papercut. Nell shrugged and set it on his desk anyway. John reigned in his frustration and kept sifting, his cut fingers locating something different: an odd, old-fashioned envelope beneath the sea of ordinary, plain white pages. It looked like aged parchment and was sealed with crimson wax pressed into the shape of a ship's wheel. When he flipped it over he discovered the words *For Yer Eyes Only* scribbled in nearly illegible handwriting, followed by the small line, *Attn: Chaplain* on the bottom. The journalist's eyes flashed. When Nell circled around again he hid the letter back under the stack.

118

"I appreciate everything you're doing, Johnny. Remember that," Nell said. He offered a candy-stained, red smile, then cantered toward the light of the newsroom. "Try to get those stories assigned by tonight; I want to get a jump on the next issue."

"Yes sir," John said.

That response made Nell's smile widen. "Adda boy. Oh, and anything even *resembling* another fish story goes to one of the new reporters." He disappeared into the clamor. "Or the trash."

John sat in the dark room as sleet chittered over his small window. He went back to his pile and unearthed the unusual envelope again, carefully peeling up the wax seal and unfolding the letter inside. He couldn't read it fast enough. He faced the wall so the page would be lit by the warm tones of the newsroom seeping into his closet-like workspace, and squinted as his eyes skated over the choppy, misspelled words and blots of smudgy ink:

Chaplain,

I knows ya wanted me to write ya by e-mail but my computer ain't too good no more and these squiggly lines kept showin up under me words.

Anywho, I was wonderin if ya was on the lookout for another story. A follow-up of sorts. Not bout the fish I saw but somethin new. Somethin me first mate Hank said he'd heard a few days back while he was out nightfishin just past the bay.

Tell ya what, if yer lookin for a fresh tale, see if ya can meet Hank and me for a little expedition sometime in the comin month. We was hopin we'd get a good look at the beast afore the snow gets too nippy.

Yer gonna need a bigger paper for this one, Chaplain. Cause this beastie is big. Bigger than Gambo.

And her name's Giganteus.

- Winslow

Lightning cracked outside. John rolled across the short room in his squeaking, busted swivel chair and covered his face. Every fiber of his being wanted to write Winslow back immediately and arrange a meeting. His mind swirled, imagining what monster could have prompted such urgency. His fingers galloped on the chair's gnarled armrest, eager to start typing interview questions, and the small window to freedom flashed blue above him. This mailroom really *was* a dungeon.

He sighed and opened his laptop, wincing at the white glow and turning down the brightness as he checked the weather, which was projected to only worsen in the coming days. *Not much time,* John thought. A notification popped in the lower right corner of his screen. *New Post on Bayfield Messenger Online.* John opened it.

Cryptid Artifacts Surface at Local Museum, the headline read. It was his new story, John realized, hidden in the obscure *Leisure & Fun* section of the Messenger's website, rather than his own column like Albert talked about. Nell had taken that away too. As he scrolled, he balked at the sight of a different picture than the one he'd chosen for the story. The photo of Milly examining the authentic leg-shell of a monstrous lobster had somehow been replaced with the posed one he'd taken of her with the Squid-Shark taxidermy.

John shut his laptop, sinking defeatedly. His compressing chair made a tired shrill as he gazed out at the bright newsroom where Nell wiped his eye post-laughter with another employee by the water cooler. He slapped his knee, patted his coworker's arm in jovial revelry, then caught John's stare. He raised a paper cup to him.

John returned a grudging nod, then went back to the pile of mail to organize story assignments for next week's issue. He slipped Winslow's letter back into its parchment-colored envelope and set it down on the corner of his desk, pausing his work a moment.

He rubbed his hands and folded his fingers, unable to concentrate. Something was pulling at him, and Winslow's words kept repeating in his head. *Yer gonna need a bigger paper for this one, Chaplain...* only to be silenced by Nell's reminder that he wasn't to be writing. He hoped Albert would recover. He didn't want to imagine what it would be like working for Nell fulltime. He shut his eyes, trying to conjure positive thoughts.

You remind me a lot of myself when I first started out, Albert's compliment surfaced.

John's fingers started drumming on his armrest again, but this time, in striking unity, the sound of clacking keys overwhelmed his ears. His eyes reopened to the sight of the newsroom's nearest cubicle, where Becci sat, fingers flying over the keyboard to enter the finishing touches for her latest piece.

You know a good story when you hear one.

John swiveled. His broken chair squeaked. He heaved the stack of story assignments to the center of his desk, then added Winslow's letter to the top. Uncapping his pen with his teeth, he scratched out his name on the reference line at the bottom, rewriting it: *Attn: Becci Hamrin.*

There's Something Out There

arped, wooden boards stiffened by freeze cracked steadily beneath the hastened boots of Becci Hamrin as she plodded over the dock, locks of tousled, crimson hair flowing beneath her cream-colored, woven tuque as winter swept in. Its winds were strewn with salty droplets of bay water that left a seal of icy brine on everything; she could taste it through her scarf.

Above, hints of snow fluttered down from frothing, white-blue clouds. Two flakes settled on the reporter's eyelashes. She blinked them away and traced their source to the overcast, as an exhausted breath puffed through her scarf and floated skyward.

"Beautiful day," a man's voice rasped. Becci's attention switched to the person shuffling at her

127

side, hands plunged in his dark wool coat, glasses fogging.

"Oh yes, lovely," she replied.

A grin cracked on John Chaplain's face as he raised a gloved hand to his lenses to swirl away the fog. His blue eyes emerged from the haze to view her. Although Becci's tuque was pulled as far over her forehead as possible and her scarf was bunched up around the bottom half of her face, John knew she was smiling. Her hair bounced as she marched ahead at the lead.

"Let's go, J-Chap. High knees."

John's footsteps synced with hers, and they strode as a unit down the abandoned, gray marina.

"*J-Chap…* Is *that* what the newsroom is calling me?"

"No, they call you the 'mailroom vampire.' "

" 'Cause I'm always working late?"

"No, 'cause you're pale."

"Oh."

Becci giggled. "Seriously though, I'm glad you could make it."

"Me too." John smiled. He smelled the chilled, salty air. *There's no way I'd miss this.* He cleared his throat. "You know, I've lived in Bayfield for years and I've never actually gone out on the bay. I never thought I would."

Becci's eyes squinched, suggesting a grin. "I never thought I'd see the mailroom vampire in broad daylight."

John smiled and shook his head. "Can we make J-Chap a thing instead?"

Heuvelmans' Landing was the name carved on a frosty sign squeaking on stiff, rusted chains from a post snarled in shambled, shredded fishnets. The reporters' legs wobbled as combers raked at the unstable beams. Moored fishing vessels teetered, equally imbalanced, their bells clanging, while a nearby seagull roosted on a post and fussed at them. Beneath the gull a yellow sign proclaiming, *Safety First!* was tacked above a deteriorated, hole-ridden life preserver.

John chattered, "That's reassuring."

Becci laughed.

An impressive, antiquated fishing boat rocked on the far end of the dock, its shadow emerging from the whiteness like ink on fresh paper.

John buzzed at the sight of it. *This looks like the place.* He turned his wrist to check his watch. *He should be around here somewhere.* As he checked the time, a rogue snowflake spiraled into his lens. He removed his glasses, wiped them clean against his dark sleeve, and when he set them back on his nose, he was met by a massive, ice-blue eye.

"Chaplain! There ya are!" The fisherman slapped his shoulder. "Where've ya been?"

"Sorry Winslow, there was some traffic," John said, although they were a minute early. "Everyone's driving slow with the bad weather."

"I know the weather's bad. My knees is killin' me." Winslow Hoffner shifted his weight on the dock's squeaking boards, hooked his thumbs in his pockets, and chuckled, then eyeballed him and added, "Seems the beasties always come out in this type o' weather." His stare flicked Becci's way, who was waving her mittened hand at him, star-struck. "Erm... who's this?"

"Becci Hamrin." Becci stepped forward. "We spoke on the phone. I work with John at the Messenger; I'll be taking the lead on this story."

"Ah, right, right," Winslow shook her hand. "Didn't recognize ya with the scarf."

"Um, that's because we've never met."

Winslow blinked. "Anywho, good ta have ya aboard, Hamrin."

Becci laughed awkwardly as the old man turned, motioning for them to follow him up the gangplank and onto his boat. She trotted along at his heels. "It's good to be aboard, sir," she said. "And I like to go by Becci if you don't mind."

"Right, right. I hears ya, Hamrin."

"No, Becci."

"Hammy."

"No. Wait, hang on—"

John put his hand on Becci's shoulder and shook his head. Becci glanced at him, her brow scrunched in puzzlement, then relented, "Hamrin's fine, I guess."

Winslow gave her a thumbs-up as he disappeared.

"*Hammy*, huh…" John nudged her. Maybe we can get *that* nickname to stick in the newsroom."

She shoved him, and the two climbed aboard.

On the blustery morning of March, 28, local fisherman Mr. Winslow Hoffner and first mate Mr. Hank Malloy graciously invited these *Messenger* reporters, Ms. Becci Hamrin and Mr. John Chaplain, on a voyage into the Atlantic to validate Malloy's account of a giant creature, resembling that from the frightful legends of seafarers--a beast that can sink a ship.

"Make yerselves comf'rble," Winslow said. "We gots a long trip comin' up."

The newcomers investigated the deck. The boards, darkened and splitting from age and moisture, creaked curiously at their unfamiliar footsteps. John ran his hand over the chipping exterior of the wheelhouse. The boat had been white at one point, he wagered, but years of fishing and exploration had left its imprint. In fact, the only feature of the craft still in pristine condition was the name, seeming to have been painted and repainted meticulously on raised letters, in lustrous, red paint:

"*The Seanna*," John read, peering over the guardrail at it.

"That's a neat name," Becci commented. "Is it after someone?"

"Anna," Winslow answered. "And the sea. My two loves."

"*Aw.*" Becci covered her heart.

Winslow squinted slightly at her. "My knees is killin' me."

"Alright!" a deeper voice with a Scottish accent proclaimed. "I think we're ready tae go, Wins." John and Becci traced the call to the flying deck, where Winslow's first mate was surveying the waves and the skies, before descending the squeaking steps. "Storm seems tae be breakin' some. I'd say we capitalize now an—" He halted at the sight of the journalists. "Ho ho! That's right, we've got comp'ny!" he cheered. "Ye must be John."

"Yes," John said. "Good to meet you."

"Haw! C'mere, you!" The first mate clapped John's hand in his hearty grip. "Name's Hank Malloy, son. Pleasure tae have ye aboard the Seanna. Yer a mighty fine writer, mighty fine."

John felt like his arm was about to pop off. "Thank you," he uttered between shakes. Hank released him and he adjusted his glasses, then moved on to Becci, removing his cap.

"And ye, miss?"

"Becci Hamrin." She offered her hand and he took it regally.

"Pleased tae meet ye."

"Likewise," she said, then pointed at him. "I've read about you. You're the man who heard the monster, right?"

"Aye, that's right."

Becci's pen clicked. As Hank ran his errands around the boat, Becci shadowed him, jotting down the answers he gave to her interview questions:

"That's M-A-L-L-O-Y. It means *noble chief*," Hank said as he gathered the mooring line. As he made his way to the wheelhouse he answered her next question. "Oh, been working with Wins for years now, we're like brothers." He stood at the helm when Becci asked him to recount his experience. "Weren't too long 'go when I heard the thing," Hank explained. "I was farther out than usual, out past the bay..." The motor revved and hummed. Hank eased the boat away from the dock, sloshing into the chilly expanse as roosting seagulls scattered and the snowflakes started to twirl by at greater velocity. Up at the bow, John stood with Winslow, watching the marina stretch behind them as the bay swept them up.

"What did it sound like?" Becci flipped to a fresh page in her notepad.

The first mate's lower eyelids tightened as he peered through the smeared window into the encroaching whiteness. "Like a shock o' thunder." Becci wrote down his description. "Loud, brassy. 'Cept it came from below. Felt like the whole ocean was 'bout tae come alive."

Becci's olivine eyes glinted. She added the details to her notes. "That sounds terrifying."

Hank cleared his throat. "Well, for some, perhaps. But no' a gallant sailor like I!"

John rested his elbows on the guardrail behind him and watched the interview from afar. Hank puffed out his chest as he steered, describing his bravery in the presence of a titan, and Becci's pink lips curled at his grandiose performance. She adjusted her thin reading glasses, brushing a wavy tress behind her ear in the same motion. Her fingertips were black with ink smudges.

"Ya love her, don'tcha?"

John's chest tightened. "What—?"

Winslow held up a printout of John's latest story. "Milly. She's a riot, ain't she?"

John had forgotten he'd made a copy for Winslow to read. "Oh. Yeah." His gaze floated back to Becci. "Yeah, she's great."

Winslow's right eye glittered proudly as he reached the photo of Milly holding a leg-shell of legendary proportions, crusted in barnacles and coral-shaped buildup. "Ha ha!" Winslow laughed. "Ya've got no idea how perfect this is, Chaplain. I need a dozen copies o' this pronto. When's it run?"

"It's not." John slid his hands into the pockets of his dark, wool coat. "They, uh, pulled it."

"Pulled it? What, till another week?"

"They ran a different version of it online. It's not the same."

Winslow's eye quivered. "Hm. Then make me some more copies o' *this* version, alright? There's a cook down the road I needs ta give a quick *I told ya so* to."

John laughed. "You got it."

Heuvelmans' Landing shrank in the distance and curtained in fog. Waves foamed like the jowls of a famished animal and lapped at the growling stern, then broke apart into popping vapors and fizz, as the Seanna banked and crested. At the bow, John squinted into the flurry. White particles billowed apart in warping, spiraling patterns around the boat, as icy winds blared like antique trumpets. The orchestra punctuated with cracking metal and hissing carbonation, as Winslow raised a fresh root beer to his lips.

"*Ahh*," he breathed, satisfied. "Crisp. Don't need no fridge with weather like this, eh?" John shuddered a chilled breath and agreed, marveling at how content Winslow appeared in the freezing temperature. His coat wasn't even zipped.

The fisherman laughed and patted the journalist's elbow, crinkling the new rain slicker he'd been given. Both he and Becci had been allotted sets of plasticky, bright red slickers and matching life vests. *This way we can see ye if ye tumble overboard*, Hank had explained nonchalantly. John swallowed hard and held on to the black

137

straps of the outfit as he gaped into the swirling, indigo currents below. For a moment, he thought he saw something beneath them: a dark tangle of massive roping shapes, furling and unfurling. He leaned in, rubbing the fog off his lenses. Surely the waves were playing tricks on him.

Something wrapped around his shoulder and John jumped back, then eased when he saw it was Becci.

"Whoa-hoh," Becci smiled. "Someone's skittish."

"You startled me," John admitted. "What's up?"

"Out there..." She pointed. A small, black dot in the distance trailed the Seanna on the starboard side. "Do you see it?"

"Yeah," John said. "It looks like another boat."

"It's been there for a while."

John squinted at it. *"Who in their right mind would be out in this weather?"* he wondered aloud.

"Besides us..."

John turned to his left. "Winslow, what do you −?"

He was gone. Across the deck, metal segments clicked apart as an old-timey, brass spyglass periscoped. Winslow lifted it to his eye. *"Herm..."*

John and Becci flanked him.

"*What do you see?*" Becci whispered.

Winslow lowered the spyglass. "*Dagnab.*" He tossed it to Becci. "Keep an eye on that boat, Hamrin."

"Is something wrong?" John asked.

"Hank, hard left!"

"Aye." Hank spun the wheel and the Seanna banked. John and Becci held on to the guardrail. In the distance, the black dot appeared to swell.

"Status, Hamrin," Winslow called.

"Uh…" Becci fumbled with the spyglass. She moved her reading glasses to her forehead to peer through. "Okay, I see it."

"What're they doin'?"

She shrugged. "Floating?" She lowered the instrument. "I'm sorry, what am I looking for?"

"Are they followin' us?"

"Uh…" She peered through again. "I don't think so."

"Alright, then—"

"Wait. No, wait."

"Hm?"

"They're changing direction now." She checked to make sure, then turned back to the wheelhouse. "Yeah, they're coming our way."

Winslow gritted, "Knew it."

"Knew what?" John asked.

Hank's stalwart grip on the wheel became tighter. "Yer not suspectin' —?"

"It's him."

"But why now?"

What is going on? John thought, frazzled. He tapped Becci's shoulder and pointed at the spyglass. "Could I see that?" They traded, and John squinted through.

In his cracked, warped circle of visibility, a larger view of the pursuing craft came into focus. A jet-black motor yacht was cutting through the bay at double the speed of the Seanna. Topping the vessel were rotating radar systems, antennae, and even a satellite dish. The equipment was state-of-the-art, and although John's knowledge of boats was limited, he was sure he'd never seen one with *this* many adornments. On the hull, the boat was sleek and featureless, save for bold, yellow letters spelling, *La Gloria*, calligraphied above a single, sharp logo of the same color. It looked like the planet Saturn.

John's throat knotted. He lowered the spyglass, wondering why that symbol seemed so familiar.

"Keep true, Hank," Winslow instructed. When an arch-shaped rock formation drifted through the snowstorm, Winslow pointed it out. "There."

Hank's ruby cheeks puffed as he pulled back on the throttle and spun the wheel. The Seanna swung, becoming parallel with the rockstacks jutting from the waves. "Easy, easy." The Seanna steadied. "Good. I'll take 'er from here." Hank sidled as his friend stepped in and maneuvered the Seanna between a maze of jags. "Drop anchor," he commanded.

"Aye." Hank scurried off, and the sound of rattling chains and splashes were heard before the boat dragged to a halt, and John and Becci watched the stone archway's shadow glide over them. Moments later, the black boat pierced the whiteout, its motor a deafening snarl, then blasted past the cloaked Seanna to disappear in the haze again.

Winslow exhaled and petted the wheel, then pressed his back against a wall and lowered onto a stool. John, Becci, and Hank grouped up with him in the wheelhouse.

"What was all that?" John asked.

Winslow blinked. "Somethin' I'd like ta forget." When the journalists' inquisitive stares only deepened, Winslow relented. "Alright, listen," he started, then gestured to Becci's readied pen and pad. "Off the record."

Becci tucked her notes away.

Winslow pointed a bony finger into the fog. "That boat out there... the people on it..." His eye shined. "They're monster hunters."

"Like what we're doing?" John asked.

Winslow shook his head. "Not quite. Some of 'em take the term *huntin'* too literal, if ya catch my meaning." Winslow pushed off his stool, grunting.

"Are they dangerous?" Becci chimed in.

"Not fer us," Winslow answered. When Becci looked worried, he clarified, "They ain't dangerous, but they ain't smart neither."

"Aye," Hank attested. "They have the equipment, but they don't have the talent!"

"How do you know all this?" John asked.

Winslow looked at him and Becci, dissecting their curiosity and concern. He smiled to calm them. "This may come as a shock, but I seen a lot of crazy things in my day."

Understatement of the century, John thought.

"But I learned a lot o' things, too. N' the main thing I learned was monsters ain't monsters. People is monsters. People with greed in their hearts." Winslow set his hand on the railing that led to the lower deck. "Chaplain, Hamrin... I wish I could tell ya this'd be a simple sightseein' trip, but it's lookin' a bit more elaborate than that, so..." His throat bobbed. "If ya want, we can drop ya off now. Just say the word."

John and Becci traded glances, but neither changed their minds.

"I've got a story to write," Becci said.

"I've got a mailroom to avoid," John added.

Winslow cracked a grin. "Then we gots beasties ta see."

John's head spun as he clopped down the steps. "Monsters... Monster hunters..."

"Yeah, this thing writes itself," Becci commented. She tugged at John's arm. "And if those guys in the black boat are here too…"

"There's something out there," John said.

"Ho-ho!" Hank shook the reporters by their shoulders. "Things are gettin' interestin'!"

The journey to reach the point where Malloy encountered the creature was slated to last approximately two hours. But, with the late-season snowstorm beginning to resemble a blizzard, the initial half of the voyage became momentarily compromised. To pass the time and revive the passengers' spirits, these *Messenger* reporters were treated to snacks and stories in the safety of the Seanna's cabin.

"What's another word for safety?" Becci leaned back from the glow of her laptop, biting her pen. "I don't like safety."

"*Hm,*" John thought, chewing on a strip of homemade fish jerky. He rested his head against the wall, chilled air rising off the clunking boards in unison with thalassic gushes and rumblings. Across the cabin, he watched Hank swing his feet from a reclined, unusual chair made from a halved whiskey barrel. He swallowed his mouthful. "Shelter?"

"No."

"Sanctuary? Asylum?"

"No, no."

"Fortification?" Hank tossed in a suggestion.

"Mm, no."

"What's all this bibble-babble?" Winslow asked, descending the ladders with two cans of root beer.

"She doesn't like safety," John said.

"Come ta the right place." Winslow handed one of the sodas to John.

"No, she doesn't like the *word* safety," John clarified. He cracked the root beer and took a sip. "Mm, thank you." He snapped his fingers. "Security?"

"That's a good one." Becci typed it in.

Winslow tapped his finger on his temple. "Makes ya sharper, don't it?"

"Oh, oh!" Hank called. "Shelter!"

Becci backspaced. "That's even better."

145

"Wait, I *said* shelter," John protested.

"Sounded better when he said it."

"In yer face!" Hank cheered.

"*Ahem*," Winslow cleared his throat. "Like I was sayin'…"

Becci shut her laptop.

"Ya ain't never seen a sturgeon like this afore," Winslow recounted, then laughed. "Well, I guess that's 'cause it wasn't a sturgeon. It sure had a head like one, though. Whiskers n' everything. So that's what I thought I had on the line."

"An' ye had more than *that* on the line, don' forget," Hank reminded him.

"Yer right. The *First Place* title was tauntin' me from ashore. Banners was flappin'. Trophies was gleamin'. Lake Erie held this li'l Fishin' Tourney every year or so, n' every year I attended, somethin' managed ta go awry."

The stool squeaked as Winslow's determined gaze swept the room. "*Not this time*, I'd resolved. *This* time, I had me lucky silver lure with me!" Winslow produced the fishing lure from his pocket. It was meant to resemble a minnow, but in its current condition looked more like scrap metal:

old, dingy, and chewed-looking, with a tinny finish, bent shape, and plain roundhead screws for eyes.

He patted the minnow's head. "In fact, this was the moment that confirmed fer me this trinket's luck, fer no sooner than it plunked in the water did it get yanked underneath. The reel went wild!" He made a spiral motion with his fingers and imitated the whizzing sound of the reel. "Bruised me real good just goin' fer the handle."

Chairs creaked as his listeners leaned in.

Winslow smiled and flexed. "Now, thankfully this was back in nineteen-somethin'-someodd, so I was even brawnier than I am now, if ya can believe."

Becci grinned. "No way."

"Aye." Winslow winked. "N' if ya can't imagine that detail, brace yerself fer this next part." Winslow got up and hunched, fighting with an invisible fishing rod. "I was tuggin', reelin', n' shoutin', *'I got a bite!'* I could almost *taste* the trophy."

John and Becci cocked their heads at his word choice.

"Might wanna rephrase that, Wins," Hank suggested.

"*See* the trophy, whatever," Winslow said. "So I pulled n' pulled. A big splash hit me, n' this glittery, whiskery face popped up.

" *'It's a sturgeon!'* I'd shouted. I was thrilled. But then, as I reeled, its body kept comin'… Its neck kept stretchin' longer n' longer, like a cloth from a magician's sleeve. *'What in the world?'* Hank saw it too from across the way. Nearly dropped his pole from his hands."

Knowing his part, Hank stood. "I shot up from ma jon boat n' shouted, *'Ye hooked yerself a damn giraffe, Wins!'* "

The journalists laughed.

"Might as well have been," Winslow chortled. "The thing stretched taller n' taller, then tilted her head n' made a sound like a whale. Then, as if she weren't tall enough, this big red fin fanned open on her head. Made 'er look like a dragon."

"A giraffe-dragon," Hank said.

"A giraffon!" Becci joked.

"Whatever she was, I knew I was in fer a ride, so I got in my seat, strapped in, n' held on."

"Ye can't ever let go of the pole, can ye?"

Winslow slurped his root beer. "Nope. I wanted that trophy, Hank, but I wanted me lucky lure back even more. So I kept reelin' n' Bessie kept tossin'."

"Bessie?" Becci said.

"Aye, that's her name."

"Did you win?" John asked.

Winslow huffed. "I might have had the judges turned around at *any moment* durin' my three minute chariot ride. I swear, I was coastin' n' spashin' all over the consarn lake like a possessed waterskier. Somehow Hank was the only witness!" Winslow demonstrated his intensity pulling at the line. "*Erg! Arg! Grah!*" he reenacted. The room was engrossed.

"Finally, Bessie sped off 'cross the whole length o' Erie in a blink. I prolly set a world record, but I guess we'll never know 'cause I didn't get a trophy fer that neither. Then—!" Winslow crushed his empty soda can in his fist. "My chair bent at its base, the line popped, and my whole boat flipped onta land upside-down."

John balked. "Gracious."

"Geez," Becci echoed. "How did you get your lure back?"

"I peeked out from under the boat, and it was lyin' there in the grass. Bessie hacked it up! I crawled out n' nabbed it in time ta see her tail flappin' under. She splashed off just as confetti flew in the distance ta declare the winner."

"Wow," John said.

"Sorry you didn't get your trophy," Becci added.

"Ah, it's fine. Turned out they was plastic anyhow." Winslow laughed and wiped a tear from his eye. "N' the fella who won caught this li'l guppy! Thought it was the greatest thing ever!"

Winslow hooted, grabbing at his side, which broke the whole room into laughter with him.

As John clapped and cheered, his mind wandered. He remembered the eye of Gambo as she surged from the water and snapped, and swimming alongside the memory now was Winslow's description of Bessie, serpentine and whiskered. He ruminated on what other wonders lay hidden out there. What the subject of their current expedition might look like, and when it might lunge out at them.

THUNK! John jolted as something impacted the hull behind his head.

Becci's smile flashed. "That's the second time you've flinched," she teased him. "What're you so —"

The same sound struck beneath Becci's feet and she started. "What was that?"

"Shark," Winslow said calmly.

"Aye." Hank reclined in his barrel-seat. "Porbeagle for sure."

Winslow tilted his head. "Could be a Dusky."

THUNK … TH-THUNK …

"What was —?"

" 'Nother shark."

"Now you *tell* me that isn't the thumpin' of a Porbeagle," Hank challenged.

"That's a Dusky nippin' at barnacles." Winslow folded his arms. "Take it ta the bank."

A beat of silence.

CL-UNK-A …

Becci glanced at the fishermen. "Another shark?"

Hank and Winslow traded less certain frowns.

151

"*Huh...*" Winslow strolled to the center of the floor.

"What?" Becci asked, suddenly on edge.

Winslow bent his knees and bounced his weight over a couple areas. The boards creaked. No other sounds. He rubbed his beard. "Huh!" he repeated.

"*What?*" Becci pleaded.

Winslow searched the floor a moment longer. Silence again. He sniffed, nodding. "*That* weren't a Dusky."

POW! The floor inclined. John and Becci went sailing from their seats. Hank spun in his chair and Winslow hopped one-footedly, making flapping spirals with his arms. When he stamped his other foot down, the Seanna smashed back to her original orientation, the walls and floors still vibrating like a struck cymbal.

John pushed off the floor, wide-eyed. Becci pulled on his elbow to get him steady, and the reporters clambered up the trembling staircase at the heels of the fishermen.

"Safe tae say we were both a bit off in our assessment," Hank said to Winslow.

"Jury's still out on the first two thumps, Hank."

The walls quaked. Knickknacks tumbled. Picture frames clattered. The crew burst through the exit and into the wheelhouse, Hank sprinting for the anchor, while the others went for the guardrail.

Where is it? John wondered, panting clouds of frenzied breaths. He cleared the fog on his lenses and peered beyond the great stone arch they'd been hiding under. *Where – ?* His mind stilled when his eyes adjusted, and the stone arch twisted and articulated.

Ice water pelted John's forehead and glasses as its shadow swung over him. Through the shade, bioluminescent spots fluxed in kaleidoscopic patterns, altering the color of the limb, even altering its texture.

Camouflage, John realized.

At his side, Becci stood gasted. "Holy –!"

Shivering tones hummed upward from below the Seanna, pounding through the boat and into the passenger's chests. The sound it carried blared like a muffled foghorn, and the water foamed as if brought to boil.

The journalists gripped their ears. The shadow skated over them again as the beast's limb coiled, dragging their sights to another rocky shape that fluxed and altered, drawing back to push out a fiery, bright orange eye the size of a car. A black, rectangular pupil quavered at its center as it inspected John and Becci.

The fishermen approached, Hank especially mesmerized. *"There ye are..."* he whispered.

The titan gurgled.

A white flash went off, and the pupil shrank into a horizontal slit. Becci lowered the camera from her eye as the mountainous monster let out an ox-like wail.

"Mistake," Winslow commented.

"Get back!" Hank hollered, scooping up John and Becci in his huge arms and pulling them into the wheelhouse as the tentacles spiraled and thrashed, generating waves that spun the Seanna like a top.

"Whoa!" their voices blended.

Tidal waves spewed from the behemoth's siphons as dark ink jetted to cloud her path. The

Seanna's spin slowed, righting itself like a compass needle and steadying with the ink trail in view.

"Ah-haw!" Hank threw forward the throttle and gave chase. The Seanna's motor revved and roared as the gap closed. Tentacles arched, snaked, and pressed as vapor spouted and rushes of water surged from either side of her mantle. "Look a' that! D'ye see her, Wins?"

"I see her, Hank. I can't *not* see her!" Winslow called back, gesturing to the tumbling mass of tentacles that blocked the horizon. The fisherman chanced a look over the guardrail at the ink that splattered the whole bottom half of the vessel. *"That ain't scrubbin' off,"* he muttered. A white flash on his right side nearly blinded him. *"Gah!"* He blinked the spots away. "Hamrin! Turn the flippin' flash off!" His buggy eye twitched at her until she changed her camera settings. He grumbled and inspected his boat further, following the blots of black up the hull to confirm that the lettering of SEANNA remained vibrant and unsullied. Winslow returned to the wheelhouse. "Keep at her, Hank."

John adjusted his glasses and watched the dark shape of the monster intensively, tracking how it undulated under the currents, seeming to have command over the waves themselves. He was captivated, not daring to blink, not daring to miss a moment. But Becci was even more gobsmacked:

"*That's a monster...*" she uttered, frozen on the image of the submarine-sized octopus, mantle puffing with vapor, siphons pumping out waves. "That's a *real* monster!"

Hank grinned broadly. "First supernatural encounter?" he asked. "Relish that feelin' lass, it's a special one."

Becci snapped more photos, leaving the flash off this time.

Snow twirled in, blanching the whiteout, and the great titan's eye swiveled to view it. Her pupils quivered as her body mimicked the blizzard, fluxing and shimmering whitish-silver. Then, her tentacles swooped under, diving and fading into the deep. The crew cheered.

"How's *that* for a story?" Hank exclaimed.

"That was incredible," John breathed.

"I'd call that a success," Becci buzzed, sorting through all the photos on her camera's screen. She sighed. *"Dang, these are blurry."*

"They're perfect, then," Winslow told her.

"What do you mean?"

His right eye glittered. "The best stories are almost—"

His crew jostled and whipped forward as the Seanna stopped short, and the shrills of scraping metal pierced the air. Winslow steadied himself, peeking out the windshield. He sneered. A dark motor yacht had collided with them.

"Unbelievable…"

Giganteus

o ya gots yer first battle scar. What's the matter?"

Winslow's words didn't quell the irate man on the bow of the black motor yacht. He howled something inaudible over the wintry gales, clawed at his dark hair, jabbed his finger at the fisherman, then pointed to the long, white scratch carving up the hull and over the boat's name, *La Gloria*.

Winslow shrugged and waved his hand at the damages. "That'll buff right out."

The man proceeded to shout at him in Russian, as John, Becci, and Hank lined up behind.

"Anyone know what he's saying?" John asked.

"I'll go out on a limb and say he's pissed off," Becci replied.

161

Hank crossed his arms. "Bit o' a conundrum, eh?"

"Quite the kerfuffle," Winslow agreed.

The man looked equally baffled by their language.

As he jumped and hollered, he waved for his superiors, revealing a yellow patch on his dark trench coat which bore the Saturn symbol. John's mind flashed to the backroom of Milly's museum and the drawer of items Winslow had donated. In his memory he turned over an antiquated navigational tool beveled with the same emblem. John swallowed.

It's all real, he knew.

The agent on the motor yacht nearly frothed at the mouth at this point.

"He hasn't breathed once," Hank commented.

"Aye, it's impressive actually," Winslow said.

In the midst of the man's ramblings a second trench coated figure stepped out to calm him, setting hands on his shoulders.

"Breathe, Conrad," he pleaded.

Winslow blinked, recognizing the voice, and as if sensing his reaction the new figure paused and locked eyes with the fisherman.

"Winslow?"

"Santiano?" Winslow's face cycled expressions.

Santiano smiled brightly and stepped into view. His skin was dark tan and his curly hair was graying at the sideburns. He opened his arms to twirls of snowfall, calling over the gusts. "Still fishing this spot? You chose a heck of a place to hunker down, amigo."

Winslow chuckled. "Ya oughtta see it when it gets cold."

Santiano laughed with him a moment, and the passengers eased. All but Conrad, who remained anxious despite Santiano's positivity. He scowled at the rest of them and slipped away.

Winslow nodded to the scuffed-up Saturn logo on the motor yacht's hull. "Gotta say, I ain't too pleased ta see that symbol," he said. "But if one o' ya had ta come by n' ruin my day, I'm happy it's you."

Santiano's smile faded. "I'm not the one leading the investigation, Wins."

163

The fisherman squinted, and before he had a chance to reply, a third shadow filtered through the haze, emerging from the motor yacht's wheelhouse. Conrad whispered something to the taller shape, who nodded in thanks and stepped to the front with a slight limp. Like the others his attire was black. The forked tail of a long trench coat flapped behind him, with the Saturn symbol displayed proudly on his chest. His head was pale and bald. His prominent nose cringed to take in a long breath, his dark eyes pierced the whiteness, and over the whistling howls of freezing gales, his calm, baritone voice registered clearly:

"Hello, Winslow."

Winslow straightened up. "Scalpy."

He strolled. "It's Sci-al-pi, my friend. *Scialpi*. Although you know that, of course. I see you've brought Hank with you." He nodded to him. "Hello, Hank. You've gotten fatter."

"Ye've gotten balder."

Scialpi moseyed, seeming not to have noticed the slight. He dragged a gloved hand along the railing. "And you've brought reporters too. That's smart."

164

"They ain't reporters," Winslow grumbled.

"Oh?" Scialpi pointed. "This one is taking notes."

Becci was scribbling down everything. Winslow swatted the notepad from her hands.

"She *ain't* a reporter," Winslow doubled down. "This is, ah, my niece... Hamrin." He gestured to John. "She n' her... husband is visitin' from outta town." Winslow shot a look their way. They held hands.

Scialpi's eyebrow raised. "Really?"

"Yep."

"Her name is Hamrin?"

"Well, we call her Hammy."

"*Hammy?*"

"Yeah. She's from Europe. Yeah. She's Dutch."

Scialpi's eyes rolled. "Fascinating." Conrad reappeared at his superior's side with a tablet. On the screen was the Bayfield Messenger's website. He scrolled two swipes to the archive of John's story. "For a man who doesn't want to be found, you sure keep a high profile."

Winslow squinted and shifted his weight.

"Oh, look." He held up a picture of the fisherman beneath the headline, *Winslow Hoffner's Incredible Encounter with a Monster Fish.* Scialpi grinned devilishly. "There you are."

"That ain't me," Winslow retorted.

Scialpi sighed and returned the tablet to Conrad. "While I'd love to keep listening to you flounder, Winslow, I have a job to do."

Hank muttered, *"If yer job's bein' a numpty ye should get a promotion."*

"Tell the truth, Scalpy," Winslow demanded.

"Oh, is *that* what we're doing?"

"Ya've got the whole world ta stick yer nose in n' ya chose Bayfield. Why?"

Scialpi looked annoyed. "We always have our ear to the ground, Winslow. You know that." He smiled. "To be completely honest, we might have believed all the strange readings we've been getting in this *one spot* were a glitch. Because..." He shrugged. "How could they not be? How could such a thing be possible?" His dark eyes narrowed on the fisherman. "Now we know. Those news stories you had published proved we were on to something."

Winslow's eye was stern. It glided to Santiano, who looked dismayed, then returned to Scialpi. Dissatisfied, Winslow repeated his question, his gapped teeth gritting: "Whaddaya doin' on my bay?"

Scialpi's lip curled wolfishly. He drummed his fingers on the guardrail, then answered, "Standard protocol."

Winslow exploded. "This is *my* home, y'hear? How 'bout ya stop playin' secret agent n' go back ta noddin' ta them corporate overlords o' yers? No offence, Santiano."

"None taken."

"Git outta here, Scalpy! Slink back ta that pit ya came from! N' take yer soulless excuse fer a boat wit'cha! Ya got no right!"

"Aye, n' ye got no hair, neither!" Hank added.

Scialpi looked amused. He clapped. "Nice monologue. How long have you been waiting to tell me off? How many years?"

Winslow seethed.

Scialpi went on, "If I had the choice I'd be anywhere else, *believe* me. This place..." His nose wrinkled. "My clothes, my skin, are all saturated

167

by the stench of your reeking bay. It's your fault I'm here."

"Smelled fine afore ya got here, Scalpy."

Becci giggled.

Scialpi shot a frown at her and she hushed. "I'll be gone once the monster is dealt with."

"Well, yer too late."

"Excuse me?"

"Beastie came n' went. Ya just missed her."

Scialpi's face stretched, eyes wild.

"Aye, and it was *amazin'*," Hank taunted. "Truly a once in a lifetime experience —"

"Shut up!" Scialpi barked, pointing a leather finger at Hank. "You. Shut up." He clenched the handrail and took a long breath. Conrad tried to say something, but Scialpi shouted him down.

"This is getting tense," Becci whispered to John.

John agreed. The air was grim, and the gray clouds above seemed to rotate above their boats like sharks. Despite his layers, he felt every shift of the wind, every change. One chilled breeze licked his neck, shivering him, setting all his nerves affright. But he felt even colder when the wind dissipated.

"What is it?" Scialpi growled.

"What's what?" Winslow said.

"The monsters," Scialpi grated. "What is it that draws them to you?"

Hank puffed out his chest. " 'Cause he's Winslow Hoffner, that's what!"

Scialpi simmered. "Indeed." He turned away. "Good to see you again, Winslow."

Winslow hobbled past his crew, setting his elbow on the rail and running his fingers under his knit cap for a solemn moment, but a sight from below made him shake and roar:

"What've ya done?!"

Even his own crew was taken aback by the outcry.

"I beg your pardon?" Scialpi said.

Santiano chimed in, "Winslow, what's — ?"

"The name, Scalpy! What'd ya do?!"

John followed Winslow's frantic gaze to the Seanna's name. The last four letters had broken off.

Scialpi scoffed, "Surely you're not suggesting I had anything to do with—"

The fisherman paid no mind. *"Scoundrel... rotten..."* he muttered, scouring the currents.

169

"Dagnab…" Something red flashed under the waves. His right eye twitched.

John offered his condolences, "I'm real sorry, Wins—"

"Bah!" Winslow shoved his hat into John's hands.

"Um…" He caught Winslow's coat next. "Winslow?"

The fisherman set a foot on the guardrail.

"No, wait!"

He dove.

"Winslow!"

"Whoa…" Becci snapped a photo.

"Wins!" Hank called at his friend as he swam for the detached signage through dark, freezing water. "What're ye doin'?! Ye'll freeze!"

Winslow puffed clouds of breath between chatters as he swam. Hank heaved a life preserver at him. "Grab hold, ye bampot. Yer insane!"

"He *is* insane," Scialpi remarked.

"Take that back!" Hank snarled.

Winslow spat out a mouthful of baywater. "I got it!" he cheered. He looped one arm around the preserver. "I'm on the… uh…"

Hank, John, and Becci reeled in the rope.

"What're ye sayin'?"

"Uh... pull," Winslow said. "Faster!"

The crew heaved.

"*Whoa, whoa!*" they heard Winslow yowl.

The rope suddenly became lighter, then drew skyward and flew from their hands.

Between the boats, a serpentine shape rose from the currents, dripping and fluxing colors, with the rope of Winslow's life preserver tangled at its highest point.

As Winslow kicked his legs and swung, La Gloria's crewmen looked on in awe:

"Dear God," Scialpi breathed.

"*Bozhe moy,*" Conrad echoed.

"Giganteus..." Santiano said.

"*Wha-ho!*" Winslow dangled. He whooped as he passed above them all, the titan's limb arching, then made a sharp U-turn and swung back to the Seanna. "*Hee-ooh!*"

"Drop!" Hank called.

The deck beneath him, Winslow released the tube and touched down, sopping and shivering, with *ANNA* tucked under his arm.

171

Hank threw a towel over him. "Yer bonkers."

"Thanks." He wiped his face. When his eyes uncovered, he called at Becci, who was snapping photos of a second tentacle writhing at the stern.

She lowered her camera as the towering arm surged up, then tipped like a falling tree. John pulled her away, just as the mighty limb crashed inches from the boat, sending an immense wave curling under them. They gashed La Gloria again, making Conrad howl, and were propelled into the distance.

John and Becci's arms were wrapped tightly around each other, their faces frozen in permanent shock. They locked eyes.

"Thanks, J-Chap."

"Don't mention it."

Hank rushed to the wheelhouse, slipping on an iced and steepened floor. As he got to the controls, the Seanna's mechanisms puttered and wheezed.

Winslow chattered, "Get 'er goin', Hank..."

"It's at the top o' my to-do, list, Wins, trust me!"

The engine roared.

"Turn, turn!"

They banked, avoiding rocks, and rode the momentum to safer water.

The crew wobbled and convened, checking everyone's safety.

"Everyone good?" Winslow shivered.

John and Becci nodded.

Hank clamored, "Yes, yes, now change yer clothes fer God's sake! Yer turnin' tae ice!"

Winslow arched a frozen eyebrow, chuckled, then headed below deck, patting the boat's signage as he left.

Hank shook his head. "So much for an easy sightseein' trip, eh?"

John and Becci started to agree, when a pulse-pounding growl rattled the boat. A dark shape cut the vapors, parting a portal in the fog where the immense tentacles of Giganteus thrashed and swiped at La Gloria's crew. The image swirled shut. A cry was heard. High above an airborne man came screaming through the clouds. At the height of his fall, he tried to catch hold of the Seanna's fishing outriggers, but fumbled, flipped, and slammed hard into the deck leg-first.

Winslow hurried up the stairs in new, dry clothes. "I heard a thud!" he announced. "Take yer bets, Hank! That ain't no flippin' Porbeagle, I'll tell ya that much—"

He nearly tripped over the wailing, suited man clutching his busted leg. It was Conrad.

Winslow's jaw shifted. "Ain't no Dusky neither."

Hull battered and still dripping with the ink of the legendary creature, the *Seanna*'s voyage was far from over. With no land in sight, the whiteout twisting into a terrible storm, and an unexpected passenger in tow, these *Messenger* reporters were called into action in ways they never conceived possible.

"Hold his leg so the bones line up," Winslow instructed.

John and Becci winced when they heard a *crunch*, and the agent's leg realigned.

Conrad screamed.

"Perfect."

Conrad's eyes fluttered open, landing on Winslow. His teeth gritted. *"You..."* he started, then tried to squirm free. "You!"

"Now he talks." Winslow held him still, setting wooden spoons on either side of his leg as splints. "We'll have ya patched up soon, just sit tight there, *ehm—*"

"Conrad Shore!" he hollered.

"Right, right. Hang in there, Shore. We gotcha."

He continued to squirm. "No! I want no help from you, *svinya!*"

Winslow rolled his eyes. "Ya can't do nothin' fer no one no more."

"Uh-huh." Hank came back with a roll of duct tape. "Such a crybaby." He ripped off a long strip and started wrapping the agent's leg.

Conrad broke into Russian again, as Winslow went on, "Seems every time I run inta these suits someone gets a leg broke."

"Aye, they need more calcium in their diet."

Conrad screamed, gnashing, "Nineteen seventy-six!"

"Beg yer pardon?"

The man's lip curled. His venomous stare honed in on Winslow. "Nineteen. Seventy. Six," he repeated. "Churubusco, Indiana. You came from woods, sprinting like madman. You assaulted me and stole my truck!"

Winslow's brow lifted. "What?"

"You punched me in the face!"

"Ye've got the wrong guy," Hank vouched.

Winslow's eyes flashed in recollection. "No, no, he's right. That was me."

"Fer God's sake, Wins!" Hank bawled.

"It was heat o' the moment! I'd just seen…" Winslow shook his head. "I ain't gettin' inta it. I needed wheels, alright?"

"Whoa, seriously?" John asked.

"Nice," Becci grinned.

"I told you!" Conrad cried. "I never forgot your face! Your eye!"

Winslow squinted.

Conrad raved, "My jaw still clicks when I chew!"

"Look…" Winslow sighed. "Fer what it's worth, I *did* say I was sorry. Ya just didn't hear it on account o' bein' knocked out n' all."

Conrad sneered, as a prehistoric roar bellowed in the distance and a shadowed tentacle sliced the fog.

"So, could ya just put this li'l mishap behind us fer today while I try n' save us all from certain doom?"

Conrad's lip curled. He leaned in. *"Never."*

Winslow sighed. "Well, I tried." He punched him.

"Wins!" Hank shouted.

Winslow shook his hand as Conrad sprawled, out cold. "No time fer diplomacy, Hank." He unclipped a walky-talky from the inner pocket of the agent's jacket. "Chaplain, Hamrin, take Shore below deck."

Becci immediately jumped in. "I'll take the legs."

"Why do you sound so eager?" John hunched and lifted Conrad by his shoulders, only now noticing the new T-shirt Winslow had changed into. It read, *I Saw the Piranhalope!* with an illustration of Milly Matterhorn's mascot on it.

"What? It's comf'rble," Winslow said.

The journalists carried Conrad away, leaving the fishermen topside. A crescent of briny wind swept over them, fluttering their jackets and hair as the fog parted again, revealing La Gloria's crew locked in combat with a giant.

Hank watched his friend's features. "We're headin' back in, aren't we?"

"How'd ya figure?"

"Ye can't ever let go of the pole."

Winslow smiled. "Story ain't over yet."

With Conrad snoring in the cabin, the journalists went back to the ladders. Winded, John set foot on the first step, but slid against the wall instead and sat dizzily.

"You good?" Becci asked.

"Yeah," John panted. "Yeah, I'm fine." His head was throbbing, and the swaying floor and clattering knickknacks weren't helping. He wondered if he made a mistake dragging Becci into this.

"I'm sorry."

"For what?"

"Oh, you know." He made a circular motion with his wrist. "The monster, the secret agents, the conspiracies."

"*Pssh.*" Becci shrugged it off. "I've seen worse."

"Really?"

"No." Becci joined him on the first step. "No, this is the weirdest day of my life."

They laughed. For whatever twists of fate had landed them there, chuckling at nothing on the creaky step of an antique fishing boat besieged by legends, John was happy. *This story has to be told.* "Hey, what ended up on the front page last issue?"

"Nell's story. Something about a road getting renamed."

"Oh. Hard-hitting stuff."

Becci giggled. "Yeah." She stood and offered John a hand. "Wanna get back to our fluff piece?" Her freckled cheeks framed a soft grin, and something in her olivine eyes melted John's headache away and made him feel braver.

"Absolutely."

"Steady," Winslow commanded.

"Aye," Hank answered.

John and Becci returned from the lower deck, entering the wheelhouse behind the sailors. John leaned in. Beyond the smudgy windshield lay clear water and white snowfall. Nothing.

"What happened?" Becci voiced.

"Are we heading back to shore already?" John asked.

Winslow and Hank traded glances.

"*Ehm...* why don'tcha blink a couple times, lad."

John followed Hank's instruction and the elements seemed to bend and warp.

He frowned. *What the...?*

John blinked again and the surface of the water appeared impeded in places, the currents chopping, and the clouds and fog above them shimmered in an even odder way. Patterned, alive. Suddenly, he saw it. Becci did too. The outline of scales moving in the vapors.

"*Whoa...*" Becci breathed.

Vortexing, the camouflaged tentacles of Giganteus rolled. And the Seanna navigated the living tunnel of limbs, banking and swerving, barreling toward the silhouette of La Gloria in the distance.

Hank glanced at the reporters. Their jaws were on the floor. "Judgin' by the gobsmacked expressions, I'd say we're up tae speed."

"Good," Winslow said. He produced the walky-talky he'd lifted from Conrad and radioed: "Seanna ta Gladys."

"Gloria," Hank corrected.

"Seanna ta Gloria. Do ya read? Over."

Static buzzed from the other end.

"Come in, Glenda."

"Gloria."

"Dagnab. Gloria. Over."

A fuzzy voice cracked through. *"Conrad? Is that – ? Are – all – ... Repeat, are – right – ? Over."*

The Seanna's crew exchanged confused shrugs. "I'm guessin' yer question is 'bout the grudge-holdin' fella ya had the beastie toss my way. He's snoozin' in the cabin. Over."

"...Winslow?..." Santiano's voice crackled through more clearly. *"Winslow, is that you? Over."*

"Yeah, Santiano, it's me. Listen, I'm comin' ta get ya. Have Scalpy pull away from the critter if ya can..."

"No good. We're tethered..."

Winslow squinted through the snowstorm. He watched the flittering image of the beast's farthest tentacle swing, and in tandem La Gloria made an awkward pivot.

*"What in the—*Ya harpooned her?!" Winslow yelled into the speaker. More static. "Hank, full speed."

"Aye."

John and Becci held on.

In the cabin below, Conrad's eyes fluttered open. He woozily clambered for a high, thin window through which he could see a shimmery tentacle furl and a massive, rectangular pupil dilate. He scrambled back in his lumpy bedding, aching. He touched a pounding knot on his face, then hammered the ceiling and screamed, "Svinya!"

A tirade of Russian slurs hummed through the floor of the wheelhouse.

Winslow sighed. "Sleepin' beauty's up..." He stomped on the floor. "Cork it, Shore! We're tryin' ta save yer crew!"

A second harpoon flew. Giganteus shrilled.

The radio crackled, *"Wins... Ach!"*

"Santiano?"

Static. No longer camouflaged, a dark tentacle swung, and the shadow of a man sailed through the clouds. Winslow nabbed a barrel-shaped item from the wall and darted outside.

The wailing agent flailed like a discarded toy, screaming through the snowfall. Winslow watched, set down the barrel, tugged on a ripcord, and the canister split open, hissing as a bright orange life raft inflated. And just as the raft's teepee-shaped roof popped it was crushed inward again by Santiano, who bounced and flopped frenziedly in the puffy rubber.

Santiano's head darted like a frazzled bird. *"What? Where?"*

Hank, John, and Becci looked on in awe from the wheelhouse:

"That was some quick thinkin'!"

"That was lucky."

"That was awesome!"

"That would have been nice!" Conrad hollered through the floor.

"C'mon pal," Winslow took his arm and helped him up. "Yer alright."

"Wins..." Santiano took his hand and hugged him. *"Dios te bendiga.* You saved me!" He shuffled out of the orange raft. "It's gotten out of control out there."

"Oh, really? Hadn't noticed."

"Giuseppe..." Santiano shook his head. "He's lost it. He's obsessed."

"I know what he is. Does he have a radio?"

Santiano nodded.

"Perfect. Now, I'm gonna needs ya to check on yer guy."

"Conrad?"

"Yeah. He's down in the cabin with a broken leg n' a swollen face. Ya can't miss 'im. Keep 'im from yammerin' a while so I can fix this."

Santiano headed below deck.

Winslow stood on the bow, watching the behemoth's tentacles coil and flow, developing a spiral-current that drew both vessels inward. Hank growled and battled with the wheel. The journalists scrambled to tasks at the order of the first mate. Battering winds blared like trumpets, the crashing waves thrummed, and pattering sleet offered percussion, as the Seanna flowed into the outer ring of Giganteus' maelstrom.

Through the wintry twists, Winslow spied a frantic form at La Gloria's bow. Winslow sneered and radioed, "Seanna ta Gumball. Respond."

Static.

"I know yer there, Scalpy. I can see ya. Pick up."

"Go for La Gloria..."

John and Becci were shimmying alongside the guardrail now to view the chaos. Winslow replied into the walky-talky, "I got two o' yer agents aboard. They're safe. Y'hear?"

Static.

"I repeat, yer guys are fine. Over."

"I heard you..."

Winslow paced beside the wheelhouse. "Well, how's about ya *stop* pickin' fights with leviathans, then?"

"*I can't do that, Winslow,*" Scialpi responded through graveled static. "*You've seen what this thing can do... I cannot allow this...*"

"And what gives ya that right?!"

Hank snatched the radio. "Ye've got no clue what yer foolin' with, Giuseppe! This ain't that wee guppy ye snagged in Lake Erie. This beastie... she's old as the sea herself. She's a legend!"

"*I'm looking right at it, Hank, I'm aware of its size...*"

"She's the Kraken!"

A third harpoon was fired. Another pained wail shrilled. A wave crashed as one of the beast's mighty limbs threw, tilting the Seanna and sprawling Winslow over the deck. He grunted as he slid, and a small metallic chime brought his sight to the bosun pipe, whose chain had tumbled from his shirt.

His eye flashed at an idea.

John remembered the instrument from his first interview with the fisherman. Winslow scooped it up and blew into it: Low, high. Low, high, fade.

No way...

Seeing the knowing look in John's eyes, Becci questioned, "What is that?" She tapped his shoulder, as Winslow repeated the notes. "What's he doing?"

John ran for the guardrail without saying a word. Becci followed, repeating her questions, but gasped when her answer appeared. Fire plowed through the depths like a comet streaking below the currents.

Becci started, "*Is that – ?*"

"Yes."

Gambo's crocodilian head cleaved the surface, huffing flame and roaring sonorously as her snout dented the motor yacht's stern. Scialpi went down as his vessel spun, and the harpoon cables snapped, freeing Giganteus.

Becci leaned on the Seanna's rail, her trembling hand shambling to remove her glasses. La Gloria was flanked by monsters now. At the bow, Giganteus' siphons gushed, dislodging the barbs of remaining harpoons in the spray. At the stern, Gambo bit on the hull, charring it. It was like something from the illustrations of vintage sea maps: waves curling in impossible shapes, herds of leviathans toying with boats. Even the sky above seemed affected by the anomalies, storm cycloning and cloudbank set alight by azure arcs of shy lightning.

"You don't see that every day," Becci murmured.

Winslow winked. "Speak fer yerself, Hamrin."

A final blow on the bosun pipe disbanded the second beast. The small crackle of flame she left on La Gloria's hull made Giganteus' limbs flux colors. The scale-like plating shimmered with a similar hue, rippling up her mantle and adorning her with gold. The shade she settled on gave her a plated, patinaed decoration.

Scialpi staggered to his feet in the creeping shadow of the colossus, eight arms glittering like priceless artifacts, ochre eyes flaring like furnaces.

He stared her down. *"My treasure."*

Winslow's voice buzzed on his radio. *"Scalpy. Come in, Scalpy."*

Scialpi groaned. "What?"

"There's nothin' keepin' ya here now. Yer both free."

Scialpi locked on the quavering, black rectangles in the beast's eyes. His own cast across the waves at the Seanna. The fog was nestling; the beam of Bayfield's lighthouse could pierce the vapor.

"She ain't causin' trouble. Look at her. It's time ta go..."

The great octopus' arms tumbled in the froth. She blinked tiredly. But the beam of the lighthouse illuminated her gold finish and set his rage alight. He set a gloved hand on the launcher.

"Gerry," Winslow's voice crackled in. He paused. *"Don't do this."*

The last breeze of the storm whistled over each man. Winslow's throat bobbed. He pressed his thumb on the radio. "Let 'er go."

Static. John and Becci leaned in. Hank looked on in worry from the wheel. Giganteus began to slip away. Scialpi radioed an answer:

"No."

The launcher swiveled to fire, just as the lighthouse's beam rotated, glinting off the sharp, metal barb of the harpoon and flashing in the beast's pupil, which shrank to a horizontal slit. Scialpi went white. "Oh—" A massive tentacle swung, struck the middle section of his craft, and turned La Gloria to splinters.

Becci kicked her legs over the stern's edge languidly, chewing her pen as the bay's ruby sunset settled on the water and gleamed off her lenses. Hot crimson thawed frosty clouds and painted its feathered sky with swathes of pink and cerulean. She buzzed at the sight, jotting the description, *Fire and ice* into her notepad, wondering how she might work it in to her story.

While in the writing mood, she cupped her mouth and called down to the orange life raft the Seanna towed. "Could I interview you for my story, Mr. Scalpy?"

Under a collapsed, flapping roof, the raft's single occupant scowled at her. He shivered and clutched a silver space blanket.

"I can put you down as *anonymous* if you like."

Scialpi chattered an obscenity.

"*Ooh*, I'm sorry Mr. Scalpy, my editor won't let me run that." Becci smiled and flipped her notepad shut. Her boots carried her over the deck and through the wheelhouse. She waved to Hank, who raised a piping cup to her as she trotted down the ladders and into the cabin.

Conrad balanced on one leg, aided by Santiano, as he addressed Winslow, "My uncle had phrase he lived by: *Resentment is chasm. Forgiveness is bridge.*"

Winslow nodded. "Sounds like an understandin' fella."

"I am not my uncle," Conrad interjected. He tilted his head. "But, you *did* rescue us. And this broth is delicious." He slurped the steamy drink, introduced to him as Hank's secret recipe. "Mm. So..." He smacked his lips. "Perhaps this one time I will follow his advice."

Winslow made a gappy smile and patted his elbow. "That's good ta hear, Shore."

"Don't ever touch me again."

"Fair 'nough."

Santiano said, "Thanks again, Wins," as he helped Conrad lower into a chair. "You're a good man."

"So're you," Winslow replied. "Though ya really oughtta consider a change in profession."

"Yeah," Santiano laughed. "Or retirement."

Winslow smiled at his friend, then scooted closer to the table where Becci typed in the final words of her story.

"There it is. What do you think?"

John adjusted his glasses and looked it over as Winslow's buggy eye quivered over his shoulder.

"*Hmmm...*" they both said at the same time.

"What? What's the matter?"

"It's good, but it still needs something."

"Aye, I was thinkin' the same."

"I left it open to interpretation like you said. What's missing?"

John tapped his chin. "A cliffhanger."

"Aye, smart!" Winslow slurped a rootbeer and crushed the can. "First rule o' storytellin'—always leave room fer a sequel!"

Becci grinned. "Alright." Her fingers darted over the keys, clacking in a new ending and polishing the final paragraph. "There. What do you think?" She turned the laptop their way, the glow washing over them:

192

Octopus Giganteus. The Kraken. Whatever name she goes by, this beast has frightened and fascinated seafarers for generations, and the personal experiences of these *Messenger* reporters upheld those claims. On this expedition, blurry photos and ink stains were all the cryptid left behind, serving only to deepen the mystery of this incredible creature. But, don't write them off so easily, because the next time you visit the shoreline and hear thunder, listen carefully; it may be a new legend paying Bayfield a visit.

John smiled. It was perfect. "I love it."

"Ha ha! Well done, Hamrin! If that don't end up on the front page, me n' Hank are riotin'."

They laughed, hushing when a *clunk* sounded under the hull.

"That's a Dusky."

Topside, Hank muttered, *"Porbeagle,"* and sipped his broth. He smelled the steam and smiled, as a second note hummed, this one more familiar.

He squinted to check the skies, seeing they were clear, then grinned broadly and toasted the waves:

"*Slàinte don mhuir*, me beastie."

The Messenger

nd that's what happened," Winslow said.

Ken Keeley's face flushed red. "Bull—!"

His mother poked him sharply as she shuffled past with a pitcher. "Refill, m'dear?"

Becci wiped the foam from her chin and readied her tankard. "Yes please."

Sleepy watched the amber fluid replenish, fizzing freshly. "I like your style, miss." He raised his cup, but passed out before they tapped glasses. John joined her at the counter.

"Glad we finally went out for drinks."

"Yeah," she beamed. "Good suggestion, Hank."

Hank laughed heartily. "Beer, entertainment…" He gestured to Winslow and Ken's heated exchange. "No better combo."

Keeley bit his toothpick. "Yer full of it!"

Winslow shrugged. "Maybe. Story comes out in a week, Keel. Give it a read n' decide fer yerself. And..." The old man hopped off his stool, eye aglitter, feet spryly sweeping the crowded space. "Tell ya what! All o' ya come back when I drop off me next catch. I suppose that'll be soon, since there's lots o' mackerel this time o' year..."

Ken groaned.

"And if ya order that mackerel, I'll give ya a tour o' the Seanna. The ink stains Giganteus left're still fresh..."

The immense crowd cheered and clapped. Kids whispered to each other about the monster and begged their parents to bring them back next week.

Winslow winked at Ken. "Ya should really up me pay fer all this extra marketing, Keel."

Ken shook his head. "Unbelievable."

John toasted to Becci. "Almost."

Carbonation bubbled over the rims as their champagne glasses tinged.

"Careful," John said.

"You be careful." Becci laughed and licked her thumb. "Bottom's up, J-Chap."

They drank.

"He's connected!" someone called. Everyone crowded around a single computer screen.

Through the laggy pixilation, Albert Nguyen grinned, healthier and recovering in his bed with his niece, Sunny, at his side helping operate the video chat.

He waved. "Hello reporters!"

Everyone responded with overlapped greetings and well-wishes. John was especially thrilled.

"I should be back in the coming days, but I wanted to congratulate you all on your incredible work. Our little paper was awarded *Best in the Province*!"

The group cheered and whistled.

"I never thought I'd see the day," Albert went on, misty-eyed. He cleared his throat. "I want to take a moment to recognize John Chaplain for spearheading what I believe to be a new direction for the Messenger, and Becci Hamrin for solidifying that vision, both of whose stories were

199

noted with particularly high merit in the committee's review."

The applauding room parted around the pair, as Nell Dunney watched scornfully from the water cooler, arms crossed.

John waved, as a random coworker hooted, *"Way to go, J-Chap!"*

Becci nudged him. "Hey-hey! It stuck."

John smiled.

Albert continued. "For this reason, I'd like you both to come up with a weekly column: updates on the legends of Bayfield."

Nell stamped out of the room.

"You got it," John said.

As the party died down, he strolled to his work station. The same old mailroom. Same old dungeon-like walls and rain-spattered window. On his cluttered desk was a package addressed to him. *Attn: John Chaplain.* The handwriting was too neat to be Winslow. He opened it, and found a balled-up Piranhalope T-shirt. He laughed and read the enclosed letter:

John,

Caught up on your lovely stories. Thank you for sending me my own copies. I'm framing the one with me in it of course. The others I've added to the file in my backroom. Here's a present to keep you toasty —

John smiled and unfolded the shirt to hold it up to himself, but as the bottom unrolled an octagonal, brassy instrument tumbled out onto his desk. It was the odd navigational tool he'd inspected the day he visited Milly's museum. *The Cryptolabe*, he remembered. He checked the note again:

I'm also gifting you that gizmo you were so fascinated by. I can't open the darned thing for the life of me and my husband says he's sick of me obsessing over it. So, here. Your problem now.

Toodles!

- Milly

John's chair squeaked as he pulled up to his desk. *Thanks, Milly*, he thought, tugging on the unopenable lid of the contraption. *I think...*

Becci sauntered in. "Did you see Nell's face?"

John nodded. "Oh, yeah."

"Someone's salty." She strolled to look over his shoulder. "What'cha got there?"

"Milly sent it to me." He showed it to Becci. "It belonged to Winslow at one point, I think."

"It probably belonged to Poseidon or something." Her fingers traveled over the lid to the Saturn-shaped insignia at its center. "Wait a sec... isn't that—?"

"Yep."

"Weird." She traced the symbol with her thumb. "The plot thickens." She pressed, the insignia clicked, and the lid sprung open. "Oh, neat."

John's eyes widened. *It's just that easy apparently.*

They scanned the bulbs, purple central needle, and the concave interior of the lid, which was etched with the words: *Property of CRYPTICA*.

John frowned at the peculiar engraving.

"Maybe we could write a piece on this," Becci suggested.

"I dunno," John said. "We don't even know what it does."

The needle quivered and squeaked, pointing forward.

Becci's eyebrow lifted. "That's something."

Suddenly, murmurs were heard, hastened footsteps echoed through the hall outside followed by frantic voices.

"Sir, if you don't have an appointment you can't enter the newsroom."

"I'm lookin' fer Chaplain I said! It's urgent!"

John and Becci stepped outside to see the fisherman marching through the halls at the protest of the receptionist. "Sir, sir!" Her brown curls sprang as she chased him.

"It's alright, Denise," John said.

"Chaplain! There ya are!" Winslow hollered. "By the by, great job on the story, Hamrin."

"Thanks."

He shifted his weight and bent his knees, his shoes dripped and squeaked. His legs were snarled in seaweed.

John gawped at the mess. "Oh my goodness. Winslow, what—?"

"Did you say Winslow?" another journalist voiced.

"What's the meaning of this?" Nell grated. "The floors are sopping—Hey!" He nearly slipped as he stepped in front of the fisherman and ordered, "You're dripping everywhere, take that jacket off at once! Who do you think you are?!"

Winslow eyed him down. His stare flicked John's way, then returned to Nell with a knowing twinkle. "Don't mind if I do." He pulled off his slimy, shell-strewn, waterlogged jacket and flopped it into the arms of Nell Dunney, whose face contorted in disbelief and disgust. "And since ya asked, the name's Winslow."

The room erupted with gasps and exultation:

"That's *the* Winslow Hoffner!"

"The guy from the story!"

A panting jog was heard, and the squishing steps of Hank Malloy entered soon afterward. He burbled, "Ahoy, folks. Oh—" He dragged an even heavier coat off his arms and plunked it into the editor's hands, oozing and cascading oceanic debris down Nell's gray turtleneck. John and Becci's jaws fell open. So did Nell's. The lollipop dropped from his mouth. "So accommodatin'." Hank grinned. The newsroom barely noticed as their editor shambled away, sloshing garments adhered to him. Hank gave the crowd a wink. "Hank Malloy, good tae meet ye."

The journalists all ceased typing and shot from their chairs to crowd around the local legends. The room filled with excited murmurs and intrigued stares. Both fishermen looked like the whole ocean had been dumped on them.

"You're drenched," Becci said.

"What happened?" John asked.

Winslow tried to explain succinctly, while Hank chimed in at the same time:

"Well, we was fishin', y'see? Little farther out than normal. When this tidal wave came."

"White as milk!"

"Carried us off a ways, but that eye—hoh! I looked right at her!"

"Big beastie."

"The momma had *two* blowholes!"

"Really big. Gargantuan!"

"Aye. But fer a giant, she was speedy. N' she was migratin', it seemed. We needs ta go back. We gotta—!"

"Winslow, Hank, slow down," John said. He and Becci lowered into seats. John took out his recorder. "Start from the top."

Winslow grinned. His buggy right eye glinted. "Chaplain," he beamed, "yer never gonna believe what I just saw!"

About the Author

Michael Thompson is an award-winning author and illustrator from Northern Virginia. His debut novel, *World of the Orb,* earned national acclaim in the *Feathered Quill Book Awards,* and his latest publication, *Winslow Hoffner's Incredible Encounters,* brings his trademark humor, adventure, and dynamic character ensembles into a folkloric fantasy setting.

For more information and a complete list of Michael's award-winning works, visit:

MichaelThompsonBooks.com